A HOPE OF PEACE

ELTA SERIES
BOOK 0

C.A. EDWARDS

For information contact: www.caedwardsbooks.com

Cover design by C. A. Edwards

Author photo by Alexa Appell

ISBN: 978-0-9953384-6-3

First Edition: April 2021

10 9 8 7 6 5 4 3 2 1

CHAPTER ONE

I spit a mouthful of dirt onto the dry ground. Gritty sand grinds and wedges itself between my teeth. The tip of my nose stings where it struck the gravel. Despite my efforts to remain on my feet, I am toppled again.

Marlow's friends stand around him, taunting me with insults, while he receives congratulatory pats on the back. His reward for a solid blow to my jaw. But his assault is far from over. He stomps forward and grabs the back of my shirt, lifts my chest from the ground as his furious breath blows against my cheek.

"Why don't you run to your mommy and daddy and tell them about how mean we're being?" he screams. "That's what you always do, Colfar."

What would be the point of telling my parents? The boys standing around me haven't responded to any correction from the adults. The boys hate me, not because of something I did to them, but because both of my parents are still alive. In the village, I am among the lucky ones. Almost every other family here has lost someone. Over half of the children have lost one or both of their parents to the war with the Nadeens. Death leaves children with only extended family or kind-hearted people in the community to raise them.

My mother says these kids are hurting, but I feel like the only one that is hurting. It is my pain that makes Marlow happy. He is determined to make me suffer. I wish he wouldn't hunt me down to beat me.

I am always walking around the village with a swollen eye or a cut lip - courtesy of Marlow and his friends. It wasn't always this bad, or frequent. It is their age and growing size that makes their beatings hurt more. They are getting stronger and causing more damage. But they aren't the only ones getting stronger. I have left my mark on a few. The scar on the right side of Marlow's forehead is from a fight three months ago, and the sight of it makes me smile. It is a reminder that I am not always the victim.

"Leave me alone," I shout, struggling to break free from his hold.

The boys laugh as once more Marlow throws me to the ground. "You crossed into our side of the village," he says. "What did you expect? A warm welcome?"

"My mother needed me to deliver a package to—"

"You should have asked someone else to take it for you. You aren't allowed here, and you know it." He presses his knee against my back. I howl as rocks dig into my chest. "Come on, Colfar. Aren't you going to fight me?"

"I'm not allowed to fight you anymore. Terrick said so." I want to. It is taking all my strength to fight the urge to hook him across the jaw. I know if I strike him, I'd have to face my parents' disappointment.

Marlow lifts his knee and sends his foot into my side. "It's no fun with you just lying there." He taps his foot against my ribs. "Get up."

I shake my head and hold my hand to my side, blocking his foot.

"Come on, Marlow," one of the other boys says. "We should go before we get in trouble."

"I want him to fight me first."

I spit out another grain of sand. "I said I won't fight you." If he sticks around much longer, I will.

Marlow laughs. "You want to. I saw it on your face." He backs up, giving me a chance to catch my breath.

I dig my fingers into the dirt. He is right. How can I lie here and take his beating without defending myself? What will my friends think?

My fingers curl around a rock, and I tighten my grip, pressing the stone against my palm. I run my thumb over its rough, jagged edges. The rock may not be large, but it will hurt.

I push my body off the ground, and they take a step back.

My side aches.

I steady myself.

Marlow smiles and steps forward, leaving his friends to wait behind him. "Finally, we have ourselves a proper fight. Okay, Colfar. Show me what you've got."

My foot slides back, and my eyes fix on his face. My arm arches back and I fling the rock forward. It soars through the air, striking Marlow in the forehead, below his scar. His knee bends as he holds his hand to his head and reaches for the ground.

"That's not fair!" Marlow shouts. "He threw a rock."

"You kicked me when I was on the ground. How was that fair?"

"I didn't use a weapon." He lifts his hand from his forehead. A dribble of blood slides down the side of his nose and pools across his thin lips. "You did this."

"It's your own fault. You kicked me and threw me to the ground. What was I supposed to do?"

"Run," he says. Marlow and his friends scatter. I am left alone, holding my side and longing for a cool cloth on my jaw.

A firm, yet gentle hand grips my shoulder and turns me around.

"Colfar March?" It is my parents' friend, Ralda. She stands in front of me with a frown on her face. Her curly and wild hair rests on her shawl-wrapped shoulders. Ralda is a confident woman and not someone to argue with. She doesn't shy away from speaking her mind, but she is protective of me. "Well, look at you. Fighting again, I see. What will your parents think?"

"It wasn't me, Ralda. It was Marlow and—"

"No excuses. You know how Terrick feels about you boys fighting. Your parents are fed up with it all, too."

"But it was Marlow."

She sighs, holds my chin in her hand, and turns my face side-to-side. "Hmm… it looks like they hit you hard."

I nod and wince under her grip. "I tried not to fight him this time. I even let him pin me on the ground."

"But you did eventually fight him."

"I did."

"And what made you finally do it?"

"I was tired of him hurting me. He kept kicking me. At some point, I had to stand up for myself. Right?"

Her frown disappears, and a warm smile crosses her face. "Well, I won't stand here and tell you what you should or shouldn't do. That is your parents' job. I am only happy to see you are in one piece. I came here to tell you your mother has been calling your name for the past several minutes. Get going before she has the entire village looking for you."

I thank her and stagger down the road, now aware of my mother's voice calling my name. En route, I am stopped by three well-intentioned women who also inform me that my mother is looking for me. I want to say I am already on my way home and they are keeping me from getting there, but I thank them and carry on my way. Not only do I have both of my parents, I also have other adults who genuinely care about me. People like Ralda. Even though she didn't want to hear much about Marlow, I know she will talk to my parents about what she witnessed and will also speak to the adults who look out for Marlow and his brother. Not that it will help, but she will try.

I have grown up in this village. It is a community where people look out for each other. The community has suffered under the attacks from the Nadeens. No matter how many times the Nadeens strike, we band together to rebuild and survive. We have carved out this little stretch of land and call it our home. The Nadeens may control the rest of Elta, but this is ours.

My mother continues to call my name as I pass the many homes and shops on the dirt road. I cross the bridge that stretches over the ravine and leads to the houses on the other side. Next, I dodge chickens that peck at a puddle. They flap their wings as I run by. A pair of adults stand near a tailor's shop and block my way, forcing me to run around them.

People walk about, gathering supplies, holding conversations, and crowding the streets.

"Hey, Colfar."

I stop and turn. It is my friend Rory running toward me. Rory and I have been friends since we were small. Some would say we still are small, but at eleven-years-old, I'd say we aren't little anymore. His parents were friends with mine, so we have always been together. He is slightly shorter than me, but not by much. It doesn't make him any less strong. He carries a cloth ball, but it isn't his. It is one of the few playthings shared by the children in the community.

"Where are you going? I thought we planned to play Tusselball after you finished delivering the package for your mom."

"We were," I say, catching my breath. "But then I ran into Marlow."

"Not again," Rory says. He narrows the distance between us. "He didn't take another swing at you, did he?"

"Can't you tell?" I turn my cheek. A bruise must have formed on my face somewhere. "I'm a little banged up. I'm not sure if I feel like playing Tusselball now."

Rory sighs and drops the ball to the ground. "Marlow acts like he owns the whole village. We need to do something, or they'll keep us trapped on one side of the bridge. There's more to do on their side of the ravine."

"All we could do is hang out inside the caves," I say. No one wants to play inside the caves. They are for shelter from the

Nadeens and are full of terrible memories. I can't imagine playing in there for fun.

A woman grabs my arm and tugs me forward, followed by another push against my back. "There's no time for chit-chat," she says. "Your mother needs you. Now, get going."

"Thank you," I say, waving to her and Rory as I continue down the road toward home.

On beating days, as I call them, I find the poverty of my community is always more visible. Probably, because of my negative mood. Sometimes I am thankful for what we have, but I can't think positively when my side and face are sore. Today, I see many of my neighbors' homes direly need repairs. Rocks or stacks of wood hold down the metal roofing, front doors barely hang on to their hinges, and some homes are too small for the growing families living inside.

My father is one of the best builders in the village and worked hard to build our family home. With its solid walls and secure door, I have never felt unsafe, or that it might collapse onto us. My father takes pride in building things well, but with so few skilled workers or people available to help, construction of sturdy homes is slow, leaving unskilled people to resort to constructing makeshift shelters on their own.

It is challenging when every few years the Nadeens knock down what we build. Airstrikes chip away at our resources and any progress we make. People are tired and some look ready to give up as they sit outside their doorways and stare at nothing.

I swing open the front door of my home and the smell of freshly baked bread greets me.

"There you are," Ava, my mother says. She smiles and wipes her hands on a towel. With her hair neatly pulled back, the few strands that escaped from her hairpin frame her soft-featured face. People have often commented on how beautiful my mother is. I think they are right.

My mother sighs. "Where have you been?"

"After I delivered the package, I stopped to watch the blacksmith. He's trying to make an engine."

"An engine?" my mother holds her position. "Well, it will surprise me if he completes it before…" She shakes her head. "I hope he is successful. Every new piece of equipment we have around here will be useful. Goodness knows, we've gone without long enough. Speaking of going without…" She shoves a bundle wrapped in cloth into my hands. "Take this to your father. And don't dawdle. I need you to get it to him while it's still hot."

The cloth is warm against my hands. Inside will be my father's lunch. I turn toward the door and my mother grabs my arm. "I guess the blacksmith didn't give you that swollen lip?"

"He didn't." I stare at the ground. I know the look that will be on her face. "It was Marlow."

"What did I say about fighting with him?"

I open my mouth and snap it shut. She wasn't looking for an answer. She opens the door and ushers me outside with a hand to my back. "Hurry, now," she says. "We will talk about Marlow later. Don't keep your father waiting."

With my father's wrapped lunch in my arms, I set out down the road, past my neighbors' run-down homes, on route to the meeting hall where my father meets with the leaders of the village.

My father has been a leader on the council for as long as I remember. Probably since before I was born. The council prioritizes repairs in the village, resolves conflicts among the people, and determines how best to defend us from the Nadeens. There are days when my father comes home from meetings looking sad and tired. Sometimes he doesn't feel like eating. It makes me wonder how hard it is to lead or if there are more threats from the Nadeens that he doesn't want to talk about.

It has been a year since the last attack. They said at the time that it wasn't a "bad one", but I remember what it was like. The Nadeens destroyed homes. They injured several people. Others died. It felt bad, even if they said it wasn't. I can't imagine what it could have been like if others have seen worse.

That day, the leaders rescued people from the rubble and helped people to safety in the caves. After days of clearing away the mess, my father spent long hours constructing make-shift shelters before resuming his work of building long-term homes. It felt like his work would never end.

These days, the council meets weekly to discuss the progress around the village. Their meetings are long and boring. I can't imagine wanting to sit around discussing how they should use land and who has been arguing with whom. My father insists that this is what most of their meetings are about, but sometimes they talk about the Nadeens and any messages our people have intercepted.

My father has been meeting with the leaders since this morning. Some days, I wonder if my father sleeps in the meeting hall. Conveniently located across the bridge, near the center of the village, the hall is easily accessible by everyone and open to the public. Smoke rises from the vent on the roof. They have the wood stove burning to keep the building warm, however, given the number of the heated conversations I have stumbled into, it is surprising they need the stove to make themselves warm.

I open the door and tiptoe inside. The room is full. Observers stand with their backs pressed to the walls and watch as the leaders meet around the table in the middle of the room.

"So, the people still refuse to move?" one man says. I don't know who he is but has been on the council for at least two years.

"They insist that this is our home, and they refuse to be driven away from it," another says. This man is Hayden and is a good friend of my father. Some would say he is one of the most respected leaders in the village, next to Terrick.

"Remember the Nadeens lay claim to all other land on Elta and won't allow us to go elsewhere," my father replies. He sounds confident, yet tired. I suspect they have been arguing this same point for some time.

The first man leans forward, stretching his arms over a map spread out on the table. "We will need more land, eventually. Our population is growing, and we will outgrow this space in another few years. Maybe less."

"We will need to do something," Hayden replies. "Perhaps, negotiate with the Nadeens?"

A man along the wall leans toward another. "The Nadeens won't negotiate," he whispers. "You know how they are."

"Can we transport people?" a third councilman suggests.

"Away from Elta?" my father asks.

"Yes. If we can't get more land from the Nadeens and we outgrow what we have, we will need to go somewhere."

My father shakes his head. "We only have the twelve transporters that Brocklund Miller brought with him when he left the Nadeens all those years ago to start our community. The technology isn't reliable, and it would take too much time to go back and forth transporting people. For starters, we'd have to agree on which world to make our new home. It would be a logistical nightmare to figure out construction at the new site with few builders and resources, on top of trying to determine where to send everyone."

"Well, we must do something," the third councilman says. "We can't keep going on like we are. Negotiating with them may be our best answer."

"Do I need to remind you we're at war with the Nadeens?" the first man asks. "Negotiating with them for more land is out of the question. They attack us when we have lived here for years. What makes you think they won't attack us after we negotiate for more land?"

Hayden folds his hands and places them on the table. "If we negotiate for land further away from their city than we already are, perhaps, it might satisfy them."

"That's ridiculous," the first man says. "I say, if this is the route we want to go, we give them everything they have ever asked for and then we negotiate."

"Are you suggesting we return everything that Brocklund Miller took with him when he defected?" Hayden asks. "Some items he took when he broke away from the Nadeens don't exist anymore."

"Then we make them."

Until now, Terrick, the most senior of the leaders, has sat silently at the end of the table. He rises from his chair and the conversation stops. "There have been many good points raised," Terrick says. "We have people who don't want to leave their homes. Traveling to another part of Elta is difficult, because of the complexity of the hike and the mixed ages of our population.

Aldon has raised a good point about the transporters and issues around leaving Elta altogether. Negotiating may be our only option."

The councilors sit silently around the table with their hands folded in front of them. Is the conversation over? Can my father eat now?

I adjust the package of food in my hands and take a step forward. A floorboard creaks. They turn to look in my direction.

My father smiles and rises from his chair. "Colfar. Is that my lunch?"

"It is," I say. I hold out the package and take another step forward.

"Should we pause our conversation and take a moment to eat?" he asks the council.

"That would be a good idea," Terrick says. "We may think clearer once we get some food in us."

My father takes the package from me and places it over a portion of the map on the table. "Let's see what your mother has prepared today." He unfolds the cloth, and a bread roll tumbles out. It dances along the edge of the table and slips over the edge. I reach out and catch it mid-air. "Good boy," my father says. "Well done."

I breathe in the smell of the fresh roll and my mouth waters. My mother bakes the best rolls in the village. People have asked her to bake extra for themselves but tending to the sick and elderly takes up her time. There is no time for extra baking.

"You're getting big, Colfar," Hayden says. "One day, you may end up sitting around this table."

"He'll avoid being on the council if wants to keep his sanity," the third man says.

The men laugh as they dig into their own meal packages. The room now smells of grease and bread.

My father gives me a pat on the back and picks up a chicken leg from his lunch. "Thank you, Colfar. So… are you going to tell me about that mark on your cheek?"

I raise my hand to my face and feel my cheeks warm. He, too, has noticed I have been in another fight with Marlow. "Mother says we'll talk about it later." I know that talking will lead to a punishment. He warned me of that after my last fight.

"And we will," my father says. "You should probably get going. Thank your mother for me."

"I will."

The men that had been standing against the walls have left. There is nothing to see or overhear while the council breaks to eat. Over lunch, they will only talk about personal matters as friends. They are no longer men trying to make decisions for the community.

I step out the door into the bright sunlight and scan the buildings for any signs of people I know. The streets are almost empty as most people have also stopped their daily chores to eat. My stomach grumbles and I set off back through the village where my mother will have more food waiting for me. Hopefully, she has saved me one of those freshly baked rolls.

CHAPTER TWO

That night, I place my bruised cheek against my cool pillow. I have nothing to ease the pain of the burning rash from where the gravel scraped against my skin. I flip onto my back, hoping to find relief from the many aches and pains inflicted on me by Marlow. My hopes are in vain. The burning and dull aches continue as I stare up at the wooden roof.

I am tired of being hurt. My parents made me promise to solve my differences with Marlow through conversation, but it hasn't worked yet… and isn't going to. I need to go back to defending myself and proving that I am just as strong, or stronger.

It will disappoint my parents, but this is how boys my age work out their problems. We don't sit around a table in a meeting hall and debate or negotiate. We pound each other with fists. My parents say there is enough violence from the Nadeens, and we shouldn't fight each other, but fights happen. They insist that since we live in the same village, we need each other to survive. That means, we need to learn to live together. I will not sit back and do nothing about it. At least, if I punch Marlow, my knuckles will hurt, and I can focus on a throbbing hand. Knowing he hurts too would distract me from my aching body. I am tired of the adults giving me advice and then watch them do nothing to fix the issues.

It is the same with the Nadeens. The council is doing nothing. They argue about an approach and end up doing nothing at all. It has been a year since the last attack. Another one will happen soon, and they know it.

I sit up and drive my fist into my pillow. In all areas of my life, I am asked to be like everyone else and do nothing. Avoid Marlow and don't fight. Why should I do nothing? I want to be helpful but can't help because I am a child. There must be something I can do. There must be more for a kid to do in the village than just deliver meals, get into fights, and be sent to bed early.

A thin curtain separates my space from the rest of our tiny three-room home. It is a visual divider and nothing more. From my side I listen to my parents finish cleaning the dinner dishes and to the squeaking of the stove as my father throws another log onto the fire to keep us warm tonight. Cleaning the dishes is usually my chore but being sent to bed early after fighting with Marlow keeps me from my responsibilities. I upset them, no doubt by giving them one more thing to do around our home after already doing so much around the village.

"What are we going to do about Colfar?" I hear my mother say from behind the curtain. "All of this fighting is getting out of hand."

A chair drags along the floor. Someone is now sitting at the table.

"I think the problem is bigger than Colfar," my father replies. "He isn't the only one who is struggling. There are bigger problems. The adults can't give these kids the attention they need."

My parents give me plenty of attention. I don't feel ignored by them. While they have work to do and I don't always get to be part of, I don't feel that I am neglected. Or maybe they aren't talking about me?

"Then what are we to do?" she asks. "Colfar is covered with bruises again."

"I saw the mark on his cheek. It will heal."

"It will, but this isn't healthy for him and it is bad for his reputation. Everyone will think Colfar is a bad kid and we both know he isn't."

I toss myself backwards onto my pillow and pull my covers over my head. Is that what people think of me? That I am a bad kid? At least my parents believe I'm not, but at what point does it not matter what my parents think? What happens when the entire village thinks I am the problem?

Covering my head does nothing to mute my parents' conversation. I still hear their voices through the fabric that cocoons me and feel sweat beading on my body.

"I will talk to the council tomorrow and see if we can do something," my father says. "Maybe we can find something productive that will help them learn to get along and set aside their differences."

"What productive ideas do you have?"

I hold still under the covers and lean to the side, straining to hear what my father might suggest.

"They could work on a project together. Help in the garden. Clean up the roadways. I don't know."

My father's idea is to make us work? I want to help and not be useless, but I can't imagine working with Marlow.

"I can see why Terrick says you're the man with all the ideas," my mother says with a giggle to her voice.

"I try."

Their conversation ends, and the lantern in the next room is extinguished. I emerge from the under the blankets. Now, I have all night to fret over what the council will say. Do they share the same concern as my parents? Whatever they decide, I hope it will help fix the problems. All I can do is prove to everyone I am not the problem.

They have sentenced us to clean the stands at the market. The council called it, "An opportunity to rebuild relationships." It is stupid. I don't want to be here with Marlow where we have to remove the merchandise and produce from the stands and wipe out each wooden box. Marlow doesn't want to be here either and has been making my afternoon miserable. Frequently, he lets water stream from his cloth down my back and other times, he knocks over my bucket. He also entertains himself by calling me names or "unintentionally" bumping into me. Never once does he apologize.

My father's idea will never work. All this is doing is creating additional opportunities for Marlow to torment me. The adult assigned to supervise us is too busy watching a young lady at the weaving shop across from us. He only cares if we are being too noisy or are making a scene which distracts the young lady from his attentions. If I complain about Marlow, he doesn't listen to my concerns, and tells me to get back to work.

The water wrinkles my soaked fingers, while my back and shoulders ache. This is not a fun activity meant to build a friendship. It is the punishment I knew was coming. I want to slip away unnoticed, but Marlow would tell someone if I left. Leaving won't help my situation any. All it would do is solidify anyone's negative opinion. To prove I'm not the bad kid they think I am, I will do what they expect of me. I will try to talk to Marlow. I'd rather stuff the soapy rag in my mouth, but I'll talk to him so I can say I did.

As Marlow scrubs out the apple bin, I edge closer. The soap suds cling to the wood and form a soapy pile on the muddy ground below.

"Marlow, I don't think I've ever said I was sorry about what happened to your parents."

"Why do you care?" he snaps back.

"Because I've often thought how it must be hard."

"So, you want to rub it in that your parents are still alive?"

"No. That's not what I'm saying."

"You still have your parents, so shut up." He swings his foot toward my bucket, and I block his strike with my shoe.

I wasn't trying to make him angry with my comment or to brag about having living parents. I hate that there are kids who have lost families. I hate that I have lost friends in the attacks. I know what it feels like to be playing with kids one day and find them gone the next. I find no joy in hurting someone by talking about my parents. That is all it takes these days: mentioning your home when someone has lost theirs or talking about your parents when there are kids who are orphans. I am thankful for what I have, but some days it feels that having something someone else doesn't causes more harm than it's worth. It strains relationships and builds walls between people.

With our chaperone distracted by the girl across the road, Marlow takes advantage of the opportunity to push me into a puddle.

"Never talk about my parents again."

"I was only trying to be friendly."

"You think it's friendly to talk about my dead parents?"

"I'm sorry." If I could take my comment back, I would. I had meant well.

"You're not sorry enough. Your time is coming."

"Are you saying you wish my parents were dead?"

Marlow shrugs and kicks my bucket across the market. The chaperone looks in our direction. Marlow leans forward. "I'm saying, at some point your family's luck will run out. Just because your father is a leader around here doesn't mean it won't ever happen to him, or your mother… or you."

My hands dig into the dirt. My family's luck could run out, but not today. I jump to my feet and run toward him.

My hands stretch outward. I reach for his shirt but am pulled backward and pushed back toward the market's stands.

"Colfar," the chaperone says, holding me still. "It would be best for you to control your temper."

"But he—"

"Don't you go blaming Marlow for your behavior. The

council gave you a job to do and it would be wise for the both of you to get back to work instead of getting into a fight."

"He started it," I say in protest.

The chaperone raises his finger to his lips and then points to my bucket across the market. "Go pick up your bucket and fill it."

There is no point in trying to explain myself. The chaperone doesn't care. I did what they encouraged me to do to fix things. Just as I predicted, it didn't work. Marlow wants to hate me.

I cross the market, dragging my feet as I go to pick up the bucket. Across the road, the young lady watches the chaperone. A coy smile is on her face. Perhaps his interaction with us impressed her. It is ridiculous, the things that impress a girl. When I grow up, I will impress no one in a way that embarrasses others and will marry a girl who likes the same things as me. She'll like me without me showing off or acting stupid like I see so many people do.

The more I have to be with Marlow, the more I hate him. So much for this being an opportunity to build relationships. They have forced us to be together when we have no common interests. We will never be friends after being pushed into a situation like this.

I snatch my bucket from the ground and toss it into a nearby rain barrel. Every building has one. Water collects off the roof when it rains and fills the barrels. Our community well and the barrels are our community's only sources of water, and we are careful how we use it.

Once back at the market stand, I resume scrubbing. This time, however, I scrub faster. The quicker I can get this market clean, the sooner I will be away from here and from Marlow. He is also scrubbing faster. Maybe he has the same idea as I do. One good thing about Marlow is he has a good work ethic when not distracted by trying to annoy me. In fact, he has cleaned more stalls than I have. I will need to step up my effort if I want to claim I did my fair share of the work. The last thing I need is for him to complain to the council about how he did everything.

I look at the market. With the vegetables back in their bins, it is difficult to know what we have already cleaned. That is another reason this task is pointless. Why do a chore that makes little impact? None of our work is visible behind the vegetables.

"Have you already cleaned the tomato stall?" I ask.

"What do you think?" Marlow says. He tosses his brush into his bucket, slopping soapy water onto the dirt.

"You've covered a lot of ground. I don't want to go over what you've already done."

"I cleaned it," he says.

"Great. Then I'll move onto the cheese stand."

I hold myself back from scolding him for his bitter attitude. How hard was it for him to say he had cleaned it?

"Do you need more soap?" he asks, standing behind me.

I take a breath, expecting another stream of water is about to be down my back as he has done many times before. Instead, he offers his bar of soap.

"Thanks," I say. I rub the soap against the bristles of my brush and hand the bar back to him.

He shrugs and walks to another display a few feet away.

"If we keep up the pace," I say, "we could have this done before it gets too hot."

"I'd like that," he says. There is no sign of negativity in his voice.

I don't know what has made him be nice, but I'll take it. Finally, there is a break from the taunts and bullying. What does someone talk to an enemy about? We have only talked about the weather and getting the work done quickly. Is there anything else we can talk about?

Now, I'm worrying. I don't want him to think about being angry or he might take it out on me. I want to talk. What topics are safe?

"How is your brother doing?" I ask.

"He's waiting for me to get done. He's mad that I have to be here, and I am, too."

"Neither of us wants to be here."

"We wouldn't have needed to if you hadn't started that stupid fight," he says.

"You started it."

"I didn't."

I look over at the chaperone who pauses from giving his attention to the young lady and glances in our direction. I fake a smile and he nods, returning to his conversation.

"I don't want to fight with you again," I say. "I was only trying to talk. I hate being stuck here as much as you do. I'd like to get along, or at least avoid fighting with each other again."

"Then don't talk about my family."

"I won't. I only asked about your brother because I know him, but if you don't want me to talk about him, I won't."

"I didn't mean him. I meant my parents. Everyone wants to ask me how I'm doing or what it's like since they died, and I don't want to talk about it."

"I didn't know."

Marlow says nothing and focuses on scrubbing the wooden

stand. His body shakes as he presses his weight against the brush. His jaw shifts. He grinds his teeth like my other friend, Hart. It must be hard to lose parents and then not talk about them. I think I would want to talk about them. I wouldn't want to act like my parents didn't exist. I knew his parents and have memories of our families spending time together. Marlow and I were pretty much friends before his parents died. Now, I'm supposed to act like they were never here and never utter a word about them. I don't know if I can do it, but I will try.

For another hour, we continue to scrub the market. Sometimes we speak, talking about which display to scrub next, or offer to fill each other's buckets. We don't talk about fighting, or about our families. We stick to neutral topics like what foods we don't like to eat and what the weather might be like later in the afternoon. How much we both dislike the Nadeens. Avoiding the sensitive topics has made the afternoon tolerable, and we have been able to get the work done before the afternoon sun has made the temperature too hot.

"Thank you, boys," the chaperone says. "I had expected the two of you to get into more quarrels than you did. The market is looking sharp. Maybe we could make this a regular thing. Do either of you feel you'd enjoy helping here regularly?"

"You mean cleaning the market as a chore?" I ask.

"Cleaning or manning the food stand. I could teach you all how to mark people's rations in the ledger."

Marlow and I look at each other. Neither of us responds.

"It's a simple job," the chaperone says. He flips open the ledger and runs his finger down the list. "All you do, is note when someone comes to the stand and mark down what food they've taken. Others will review what has gone out and will determine if the ration distribution has been fair. Your job would be only to mark it down." He stares at us with a smile. "It isn't a hard job. It would definitely be something to do and might help you stay out of trouble."

"We don't need a job to stay out of trouble," Marlow snaps.

The chaperone laughs. "That's not what I heard. The two of you have been coming to blows for some time. This was an opportunity for the two of you to be in the same space and do something productive. It looks like you survived the day. Not only did you not cause me much trouble, but you also seemed to get along with each other by the end of it all. I'd say this was a success."

Marlow stares at the ground. I shrug. I wouldn't call this a success. We just got the job done.

CHAPTER THREE

The next morning, free from any consequences and having my daily chores completed, I walk toward a nearby trail with my friends Rory and Hart. It is a trail we walk almost daily, which leads to the viewpoint that overlooks the open valley outside of the village. From there, we can look down on the people working in the village below. We have spent hours at the viewpoint and have claimed the spot as our own. Rarely do the adults go up there when their responsibilities are in the village. At the viewpoint, my friends and I have no expectations on us. We are free.

The trail weaves between the slender trees. After years of trying to shield the village from harsh winds, broken and jagged branches protrude toward the path. Past the trees, the trail slopes up the cliffs surrounding the village. There are many worn trails that encircle our community used for conducting patrols. Other paths branch off toward water wells, the gardens, or the animal pens. There are even lesser worn trails that lead out of the village.

Leadership seldom uses them. It is only when the council needs to investigate activity by the Nadeens that someone travels outside the village. No one wants to risk the consequences of angering the Nadeens by crossing outside the village boundaries.

By regularly taking a trip up to the viewpoint, our trail should be one of the most worn, but remains slightly overgrown as our small bodies fit through the narrow openings between branches. Our footprints are the most noticeable in the powdered dirt around the stones embedded in the ground. The climb was harder when we first started coming back when we were small. Now, we run up the incline, each trying to be the first to the top.

"Out of my way," Hart shouts. Larger than both of us, he pushes past Rory and laughs as he runs by.

Rory picks up his pace and tugs on Hart's shirt, pulling him back behind him. "You're not getting past me."

"I will. You are too slow."

"Am not," Rory says. His foot slips and he falls forward on the trail, his hands flailing in front of him.

Hart laughs and leaps over him, dashing up the trail. "You are now," he calls over his shoulder.

I pause, helping Rory to his feet who then continues his run up the hill even faster than before. Quickly, he closes the gap between himself and Hart. They laugh as they bump into each other and try to knock the other off his feet. I run faster and join in, trying to gain the lead position. The trail narrows ahead, where only one person can be at the front. Another surge by Hart and he overtakes Rory. A few more feet and Hart takes the victory of being the first to the top of the trail.

He cheers and raises his fists into the air. "Told you. You're slow." Hart leans over and braces himself against his knees, panting and cutting short his celebration.

"I would have had it if I didn't have that slip," Rory says.

"We'll never know now," Hart says between breaths.

Although we have marched up this trail many times before, running uphill always makes us short of breath. I stretch my back, then walk over to the edge to look out at the village. How I love this view. Below, I see the village nestled between the cliffs of the valley walls. In the distance are the expansive, open fields and rolling hills of Elta. The beautiful green grasses across from us look inviting. We will never live there. Not if the Nadeens keep forcing us to stay between the protective walls and caves of the valley. They keep us penned here like animals.

It is a waste not to use the fields across from us. The lush fields would be perfect for grazing animals, but we can't use it. If we dared try to enlarge the village, the Nadeens would strike down our efforts and quickly make us regret ever attempting to expand. Yet, the council is considering it. Negotiating is a risk.

"It is looking even greener over there today," Rory says. His hands on his hips, he stands with confidence looking out at the land. "I wish we could walk on it one day."

"Wouldn't that be something?" I say. "I would love to explore those hills. Who knows what we could find over there? There is nothing exciting to see over here with our dirt and rocks."

"We have trees," Rory says. He always finds a positive.

I shrug. "I'm tired of the same trees. I want to see more of the world. Elta is bigger than our little valley. There are the Klarish Mountains to the east and the dam the Nadeens built to the north. We can see this land to the south and the west. While the Nadeens live to the northwest, there are the Great Plateau and the dry lands we could visit without coming near the Nadeens' city. I've heard my parents talk about these places, but it seems I will never get to see them."

"Maybe one day we'll get to see more. Didn't you say you heard the council talk about negotiating for more land from the Nadeens?"

"They didn't sound confident they would be successful. They are afraid to ask."

Hart sighs. "They will have to. The gardens aren't producing as much food anymore. The gardeners were talking about cutting down more trees to expand it, but the trees make this place tolerable. Fewer trees would make it hot and ugly."

He is right. Without the trees, there would be nothing but dry valley walls surrounding us. The trees make it comfortable to live here and nice to look at.

I face the east side of the village. They could cut down a few trees and expand the garden to the east. Still, I would hate to lose more trees. I enjoy climbing them and some trees grow fruit. They would need to be careful when selecting which ones to remove.

Hart bends down and picks up a flat stone from the ground. "Do you know what I'm thinking?"

I smile. I know exactly what Hart is thinking. He is issuing another challenge. Not only do we compete to see who can get to the top of the trail, we compete to see how far we can throw stones into the village. Throwing rocks from the viewpoint, we watch them fly and land on the rooftops of the homes and shops below. Our activity never causes damage. They would ban us from the viewpoint for sure if that was the case.

At the end of the match, we crown each other with the

honor of being the best distance thrower. Since Hart has already beat us to the top of the trail, I am determined not to let him win a second title.

We line up at the edge of the viewpoint. My toes remain at a safe distance away from the sharp drop. My mother would want me to stand further from the edge, but she's not here to pull me back, and the others aren't shying away from the drop. Every inch counts.

Hart arches his back and tosses the rock into the air. It soars upward and drifts down toward a row of homes. The stone misses the rooftop and disappears from view. Most likely, it has landed in the dirt.

"Nice try," Rory says. He laughs and picks up a stone for himself. "You won't win with throws like that."

"I'd like to see you do better," Hart says.

"I will." Rory reaches back and flings his rock toward the village. I track it, watching it fly against the gray sky.

"It's going down," Hart shouts.

"Not yet," Rory says with a grimace.

"Down it goes."

As if hit by a gust of wind, its momentum abruptly stops and the rock plummets toward the ground.

"No." Rory holds his hand to his forehead. "It was a good throw."

"Not as good as mine," Hart says. He lets out another laugh.

Rory's stone also misses a rooftop and disappears behind a home. "You're up, Colfar."

I search around my feet for a good-sized rock. Finding one, I dust off its surface and roll it between my fingers. It is a good weight. Its smoothness will allow the rock to travel far. I only need to improve my aim to beat them. Since they have both missed, they are scoreless. The straightforward choice would be to hit a close target and earn the only points for this round. I don't need the greatest distance. All I need is to not miss.

I lean back and swing my arm forward, releasing the rock into the air. It arches toward the sky, but its arch might be too much. I want it to go straight. My throw seems to be enough though as the stone flies over the space where Rory's rock had fallen. It drifts downward. I crouch, keeping close watch on the rock as it nears its target. Only a foot to go.

And it disappears.

I missed. It never touched the roof.

Hart and Rory cheer.

"I almost had it," I shout. "I thought I clipped the roof."

"You clipped nothing," Rory says.

"It might have clipped a bug." Hart snorts as he laughs.

"You didn't do any better," I say.

"I will this time," he says. "I was just warming up."

Once again, Hart stands tall and arches his arm back. He flings the rock, and it flies toward the village. It continues forward, passing Rory's rock and mine. It flies another foot and falls short of his first throw.

"That should have gone further," he says, stuffing his hands in his pockets. "Rory, your turn."

Rory grabs a rock and heaves it. This time, the stone goes further than the first and lands in the middle of the roof of the blacksmith shop. The metal roof rings as the stone strikes.

"Yes." Rory leaps in the air in celebration.

I take another stone and rub it along my pant leg. "Do you think I can hit the meeting hall?" I ask.

"Do you think you should?" Rory asks. "Isn't your father holding a meeting in there?"

"Oh, come on." Hart plunks himself onto a large flat rock. "They are always in there having meetings. We can't limit ourselves because of that. If Colfar wants to attempt it, let him. He won't hit it, anyway."

I laugh and stand, pivoting to align myself with the meeting hall.

Rory leans toward me. "Didn't you say they're talking about what to do about the Nadeens? About getting more land? I don't think we should disturb them."

"We're just throwing a rock onto the roof. How disturbing can that be?" I say, holding the rock over my shoulder. "I'll only do it once."

"They'll know it was us," he says.

"So?" My muscles twitch, ready to launch the rock in my hands. I am growing impatient. Maybe Rory's expression of doubt is his way of getting inside my head so I have a bad throw. He is in the lead and if I miss, he wins. He might say anything to protect his lead.

"Your father asked us before to stop targeting the meeting hall," he adds. That is true. My father has asked that. Rory's eyes plead with me. He grips my throwing arm. "Pick any other roof. Just leave that one alone."

I study the village and the number of rooftops within reach. In the days before, we have hit all the easy targets. I don't want to target them again. I need a challenge and the meeting hall is the obvious choice. But Rory is right. My father has spoken about leaving them to do their work without the distraction of our "silly games". He said the sound of the stones striking the roof pauses conversations and makes the leaders listen for threats around the village. When anxieties are high, the councilors become concerned the stones are a sign of approaching Nadeen motherships kicking up stones onto buildings. There is always a gust of wind before we hear the roar of their engines.

I hate the Nadeen motherships. They are large, dark aircraft with undersides that open to release smaller and faster aircraft. They transport foot soldiers, dropping them off near their targets. I have never seen Nadeen soldiers near the village, but my father has told me stories about them. While the motherships themselves tend to not cause damage, what they release does. Knowing what they carry, the sight of a mothership is terrifying.

Today, the skies are clear. There are no Nadeens. I shrug off a shiver from my spine and refocus on the task ahead. I will throw this rock and I will win. This is my last chance. The game will end after I hit my target.

Rory's pleas echo in my mind. It isn't as though we are each going to take turns targeting the meeting hall like we have done in the past. My father will forgive a single rock.

"I'm going to do it," I say.

Rory places his hand on the top of his head, while Hart rises from the ground and claps.

"I need to see this," Hart says. "We've only been able to make this shot twice. Given you missed your first target, you won't make the shot today."

"Trying to get inside my head, Hart? You know if I hit it, I take the title."

"You won't hit it. The title belongs to Rory this time." He looks over to Rory, who has a slight smile. Rory isn't reveling in his potential win. He doesn't want to get in trouble and his attempts to persuade me away from targeting the meeting hall appear to be genuine.

I lean back and wait. A light breeze swirls around my ears. If I time it right, the wind will carry the rock an extra few feet. My ears whistle as the wind increases. I lean back further and toss the rock forward. The rock flies over the homes and shops and descends toward the meeting hall.

Hart shouts. Rory rubs his cheek. I rise.

The metal roof rings. Hart and I celebrate while Rory keeps his focus on the building.

"Are you being a sore loser?" Hart asks.

"No," Rory says. "I'm waiting for them to come out."

The door of the meeting hall swings open, and our celebration ends. My father stomps outside and down the road, turning toward the end of the village and the mouth of the trail.

"Oh, no." My mouth dries.

Other council members are outside, staring up at the viewpoint. We slink back out of their sight. The elation of my win is already evaporating under their gaze.

"I told you it was a bad idea," Rory says.

"I didn't think he'd get that mad." I walk over to the flat rock that Hart had been sitting on and sink to the ground. "Sorry, guys. Maybe you should go."

Hart shakes his head. "We're all in trouble and I'd rather wait here than run into your father on the trail."

"I was the one that threw the rock."

"I encouraged you to," Hart says, lowering himself to the ground beside me. "Rory should be the one to leave. He tried to get you to stop."

"I'm not leaving." Rory takes a seat on the opposite side of me and lowers his head. "We were all playing the game."

I sigh. They could run and hide in the trees to avoid hearing my father's lecture, but they are staying to remain by my side, even though I am the one that has caused the trouble. I didn't think about our friendship when I threw that rock. I didn't think about the council and the work they are trying to do. I never thought about the consequences for my actions. I thought only of the win. I made a stupid choice. Who cares about the title now? The win wasn't worth it.

"I hope you boys are happy," my father says, standing at the mouth of the trail. With his hands firmly placed on his hips, his chest expands and contracts as he tries to hide the exhaustion on his face. At the pace he left the meeting hall and climbed the hill, I am not surprised he is out of breath.

I rise to my feet. "I'm sorry, father. I was the one that threw the rock. Rory tried to get me to choose a different target, but I didn't listen to him."

"Or me. Or the council," my father says. His eyebrows furrow and he lowers his chin. "We talked about this many times, Colfar. When we are in the middle of a meeting, we can't have rocks hitting the roof. People are on edge in there. We're coming up with solutions to problems and we don't need kids throwing rocks because they want to play a game."

"I said I was sorry."

"Sorry isn't enough anymore, Colfar." He stomps toward me and stops a few feet from where the others sit. "All of you boys are in trouble. You will go home and wait to hear what the consequence will be for disobeying the council's instructions and distracting us from our meeting. I have protected you boys long enough. It is time you all understand the impact of what happens when you don't listen to the council."

"Rory didn't—"

My father raises a finger to his lips. His face reddens as he spits out his words. "Now is not your turn to speak. I will decide what is fair, not you. All of you, get moving."

I haven't seen my father this angry in a long time and when I have it was usually over a conversation with the council and never directed at me. I have disappointed him by fighting with Marlow, and now this.

This has shown him I am a disobedient and careless child. If only there was a way I could show him I am sorry and want to do what is right. If only I could do something meaningful instead of showing him I'm a stupid kid.

One day, I'll get that chance.

CHAPTER FOUR

Alone in my room, I sit on my bed, listening to the noise of people outside while I wait for my father to finish his meeting. Occasionally, I hear laughter from children playing, or adults in conversation. The striking of metal-on-metal rings out as men work to build homes nearby.

A foggy window separates me from the outside. I don't get to be a part of any activities. I am stuck in my room, waiting to hear what consequence my father will give me. My palms sweat and my stomach churns. From time to time, I alternate between no emotion and fighting back tears. When I threw the rock, I never expected that level of disappointment from my father. Neither did I count on hurting my friends. My emotions are beating me up.

"Aldon," I hear a man call outside. My father must be nearby.

Their voices are low. While I can hear the mumbles through the wall, I can't make out what they are saying. Shortly, my father will be inside talking, and I will be listening. As long as I can hear them talking, I know I have time before my impending lecture.

I straighten my back and look around my room. I hope it is clean enough for him. The last thing I need is his additional disappointment over me not taking care of what I have. My room is only big enough to fit my bed and a chair. I have tucked my clothes in boxes under my bed where they belong. That should satisfy him.

The front door opens, and I hear my father's boots cross the floor. I take a breath and follow it with a sniffle. I don't want to cry in front of him, however, I can't help but wonder if he wants me to show him what I'm feeling inside. Then again, he could also want me to show him I'm strong. Crying would make him think I'm weak and I want to be a person my father can count on. That both of my parents can count on. I want to be like them and help my community one day. He won't give me opportunities if I am a weak, irresponsible child. I have to show my father, and others, that I'm capable. If only I didn't make such stupid mistakes.

I hear my father take a breath and he steps around the curtain. "Colfar. I'm happy to see you are in your room like I asked." He pulls the empty chair away from the wall and places it beside the end of my bed. "I was very disappointed today. After we asked you to clean the market with Marlow, I had hoped I wouldn't have any further trouble from you."

I nod and look down at my bedsheets. "I'm sorry."

"Saying you're sorry will not be enough this time, Son. I asked you to not throw rocks at the meeting hall roof. Why did you do it after I asked you not to?"

"We were playing. Rory had the longest shot, and I wanted to beat him. He told me not to throw it at the meeting hall and to pick another target, but I knew I could make the shot. I wanted to win."

"Was winning worth disobeying?"

"No. It wasn't."

"That's the thing. You only think about what is happening now and not about what someone has told you. It is impulsive, Colfar. You need to think things through and weigh the consequences. Acting without thinking will always get you into trouble. It is a lesson even adults need to remember."

At the viewpoint, I had thought it through and imagined my father would forgive me for it. It was only one throw. One little rock. "It wasn't as if all of us threw rocks. When you talked to us before, it was because we kept throwing rock after rock. This time, it was only me."

"It doesn't matter how many of you threw rocks at the meeting hall. I asked all three of you not to do it. You disobeyed."

"It's a stupid rule." I cross my arms.

My father raises an eyebrow. "Is it? We are looking after this community and are making decisions that will impact people's lives. There is no room for distraction. You disturbing our conversation means we weren't able to complete our conversation today. My son interrupted our discussion. When I want people to listen to what I have to say, they will not respect me if my son is outside chucking rocks at the meeting hall roof."

"Why do they care if it was me?"

"Because, if you don't respect me, neither will they. If you are causing trouble, they will wonder how I can lead them if I can't even control my child."

I hadn't realized that my behavior reflects on my father. I didn't think I was doing anything terrible, such as wrecking things. I was playing an innocent game with my friends. There are other kids out there that are stealing and shouting rude things at adults. Some council leaders have kids that are doing far worse than I am. This is an unfair overreaction.

"What do they want you to do to me?" I ask him. We might as well skip to the consequence.

He looks down at the floor. "They don't really have any suggestions besides to discipline you."

"I did nothing besides ignore what you said before."

"That's just it. You ignored me. Am I supposed to ignore what you did? You can't be going against the leadership in the community. When we say not to do something, you need to not do it."

"I'm sorry. I get it. I'll listen and won't ignore you again."

He smiles and folds his hands together. "I will not give you a consequence over this, Colfar. I am, however, going to give you a chance to prove that you will listen to what I have told you. Consider it your last chance. I also feel it is time to do something constructive with your time. I'm not sure what it will look like yet, but you need something to do."

I groan. With my luck, he will suggest I do more work. He could volunteer me to manage the market stand, like the chaperone had suggested. That would be boring.

"You have a lot of free time," my father says. "That free time has created an opportunity for you to get into trouble with Marlow and now this. If we give you something to do, you might not have as much time to run into situations that are unhelpful and problematic for you."

"I'm not looking for trouble."

My father chuckles. "I'm sure you're not, but perhaps, it is time for you to do something productive with your time. What do you want to do around the village?"

"What do I want to do?" I pick at the dirt under my fingernails. I'm not sure what I want to do. All I know is I want to do something helpful and not something like chores. "I want to do what you do."

He smiles again. "Why?"

"Because… people respect you."

He leans back in his chair. "And people don't respect you?"

"No… they don't."

"Why do you think that is?"

Why do I think people don't respect me? I don't have to think about this question long. "Because I'm a kid."

"That's not it." My father drags the chair beside my bed and sits next to me. "It took time for people to respect me, and it wasn't because of my age. I've made my own mistakes, and I had lessons I needed to learn. Colfar, if you want to be someone that the community respects, you can't be fighting with people. You need to resolve conflicts by listening and hearing others' concerns. You must stop thinking about what you want, or thinking you have the right answer. Consider the role of the council for a minute. We weigh what we hear from the people, understand what the village needs, and then we make the best long-term decision. It isn't an easy role, and not every decision is popular in the community. We share in the decisions we make so that the people understand that we are all in agreement for what is good. One person doesn't dictate what happens. That is what the Nadeens do. They have one leader making all the decisions. We don't run the community that way. We consider others and we collaborate. That means listening and putting others first."

My father speaks with a passion in his voice. When he has spoken about meetings, he has always sounded tired, and I have wondered if he regrets being on the council. Today, he sounds different. As if he has a renewed energy or purpose.

"Do you like it?" I ask.

"Being on the council is hard work, but it isn't all I do to help the community. My position on the council is a role I take seriously, and I view the people in the village as part of our family. We have been through multiple hardships together and that will continue to for many more years. We need to take care of each other, Colfar. I make every decision carefully because I understand the ramifications of poor decisions. You need to be thinking about that, too. Even at your age. Every decision you make impacts this community. Have you thought about that?"

I shrug and shake my head. I never thought people really cared about what I do. My job is to keep my room clean and help my parents. I have always wanted to do more and have hated standing on the sidelines while everyone else does the jobs that earn them praise. People always labeled me as too small or too young. I'm tired of being a child and not affecting anything.

"I'm a kid. Nothing I do is of any real importance."

"Is that what you think? Your actions are important. If the kids distract the parents with their fighting, that is a problem. That makes more work for us. When you keep the peace between you and Marlow, that leaves your mother and I—"

"To deal with important stuff." I sigh.

"That wasn't what I was going to say. You are important. When we know you are safe and getting along with others, we can focus on what we need to do in the community without feeling guilty or worried."

"I know what you do is important. I want to do what you're doing, but I'm always told I'm a kid. You won't let me do it."

"I'd like to have your help and there will come a day when I need it."

"But if I don't learn how to help you now, how can I help you when you need me?"

"For you to help me, you need to learn now how to take care of yourself. That means, controlling your emotions and thinking about what it takes to make smart decisions. Take care of yourself first. That is important."

"But didn't you say other people come first?"

My father leans forward in his chair, resting his elbows against his knees. "When I say to take care of yourself first, I mean watch out for your safety during attacks. Don't put yourself in danger and make yourself a potential victim, or you are of no use to anyone. But don't be selfish either. Make others comfortable before you do the same for yourself. Leaders need to watch how they feel and be self-aware. If we can't think because of our emotions, we make poor decisions. We are useless if we fall apart. But Colfar, you need to examine your attitude. Learn how to manage your emotions. You can't be fighting with people in the community. You can't hate the people you are caring for. You need to love them the best way you can. If you are fighting with Marlow, you can never lead him. You must always try to work things out with those who oppose you."

Why does everything have to come back to Marlow? "I

talked to Marlow the other day, while we were cleaning the stalls."

"That is great. What happened after you talked?"

"Nothing, really. He left to go be with his brother. He said he doesn't want me to talk about his parents. He wants to pretend like they never existed."

"I'm sure that's not exactly what he wants, but if he prefers for you to not talk about them, you need to respect that."

"I didn't talk about them after he told me. We talked about boring stuff like what is happening around the village and about the weather. There is only so long I can talk about that, though. We have nothing in common."

"I'm sure you'll find something if you talk long enough."

I shrug my shoulders. "I don't think we'll be talking much. We will probably just avoid each other from now on. Neither of us wants to clean the market again."

"I am glad the two of you spent time together. That is a step in the right direction."

It isn't really a step in any direction. It was a waste of time. They got us doing a chore, but it helps no one around the village… unless my father believes it kept us from being a distraction to him.

"When can I help you?" I ask. "Since I tried to fix things with Marlow, then I showed you I'm willing to not hate people."

"Are you wanting to help because you think it will make me happy, or are you doing it because you want to help the community?"

With no more dirt left under my nails to clean, I pick at the lint on the blankets. I want respect and I want my father to be proud, but there is so much my community needs. I've heard my parents talk about it. I know the problems the people in the village are facing, and the adults have kept me from helping to find solutions. I have ideas. They might feel my ideas aren't good enough, but I want to have them heard.

I see the sick people and am not blind to the issues. The problems are everywhere. People are missing limbs from previous attacks. Families are without parents or children. The selfish part of me wants the satisfaction of having done something. I don't want to sit and observe.

"Is it to make me happy or to help the community?" my father asks, again.

I look up at him. He is strong. Not just physically, but mentally. He has done so much for the community in his lifetime. He has sacrificed his time and his health to serve. He believes he can make this place better and doesn't do it because he is selfish or for praise. If he did, he would have quit by now as others have done. My father takes the good and the bad. I've watched people stop him in the street to complain about decisions the council has made. They have discouraged him, but he has never let that stop him. I admire him, but that is not why I want to help.

"It's not to make you happy," I say.

"So, why do you want to help?"

I feel my throat tighten. Tears fall down my cheeks, leaving wet circles on the surface of my blanket. "I want to make things better," I squeak. "I've delivered food for mother and seen the hurt and sick people. You do a lot around the village with the council and with repairs. I want to do more to help our community survive and grow. One day, I might need to fight the Nadeens or help those they hurt. I want to be ready and not sit back and watch people be sad. I don't want to do nothing when I see scared little kids. I… I want to help."

My father takes my hand. "I hear you," he says. Finally, someone is listening. "One day there will be peace between us and the Nadeens. We must always try to think of ways we can unite Elta. It will come. I appreciate you have a heart for wanting to help. I will continue thinking of ways you can be a part of the work around the village." He smiles as he stares into my eyes. "I think there will be areas where you can come alongside us. Please, remember what I said about taking care of yourself. While we can do our best, we can't help everyone. That includes Marlow. We can only do our best. There is a lot of suffering, but there is a lot of good here, too. Think about what you like about the village and the happiness we share as a community. You might surprise yourself when you realize what we already have."

I look up at my father and smile. "I'll try."

CHAPTER FIVE

"Colfar, take this to your father." Like every other day, my mother thrusts my father's bundled lunch into my hands, and I rush out the door to deliver it to him while the meal is hot.

As I run past the mix of shops and homes, the smell of other savory meals fills the air. Workers and families have taken a break from their activities to eat. I reach for the handle on the meeting hall's door and slip inside. The room is relatively empty, aside from the councilmen seated around the table. Hardly anyone has come today to observe the conversation. As usual, they have spread out a large map over the table. Someone has placed stones on various spaces where there is flat land. I stand along the back wall in a darkened corner. I'm sure they know I'm here, but I want to listen as long as they will allow. To learn.

"We need more land," states a man with a mustache from the end of the table. "I've done the assessments and run through all of our options, I wanted to see if the soil to the east can sustain us or if we can build on the slopes. What I discovered is if we cut trees to make space, it will worsen conditions for the crops we already have. The crops need shelter. The slopes make little sense as they are too unstable with erosion."

"What about having people live inside the caves?" another man states.

"Who wants to live in there?" another says. "The conditions are dark, cold… sometimes damp. It's not a long-term solution for anyone."

"No one goes into the caves other than to seek shelter during an attack," Hayden says. "It wouldn't make anyone comfortable living in there. It is hardly a home."

My father sits forward and slides his hands over the surface of the map. "I agree the biggest concern is finding land to produce more food. We need to grow more and raise more, and we can't grow food in the caves."

The councilors nod their heads in agreement, and I can see their point. There is no natural light in the caves. It is dark when we don't turn on the lights we have hung inside for emergencies. Nothing would grow in there.

Terrick rises from his seat at the end of the table. "Aldon makes a good point. The caves, while not ideal for accommodations, are not an option for growing food. If we need to use the caves for temporary housing, that is what we must do, but we still need to come up with a solution for food. It would be helpful if we could re-purpose land we already have homes on, but we can't displace anyone when we have no place for them to go. We keep coming back to a lack of extra space."

Why does the council keep talking about spreading out onto unused land? I have heard them tell stories about the Nadeens' city. There, they stack homes and people live in rooms above others. The Nadeens use the same patch of land to support four or five stacked homes. Why couldn't we do the same?

"Could we make the houses taller?" The councilmen turn to look at me. I hadn't realized the words had slipped out of my mouth. I hold out my father's lunch to distract from my disruption, and my father waves me over.

"Go on," my father says.

"Home?"

"No. Tell us more about your idea."

My heart beats faster. He wants me to address the council. I swallow away a lump in my throat. "I remember hearing how the Nadeens have tall buildings that are homes for multiple families, all stacked on top of each other. Could we do the same thing? Would we need more land then, or could we re-purpose the land where a house is no longer needed?"

My father and Terrick look at each other as councilors mumble. I place my father's lunch on the table, careful not to bump any rocks on the map, and take a step back. He grabs my shoulder.

"Thank you, Colfar. That was an option we hadn't considered yet. Why don't you stay for a little while and leave when you're tired of listening?"

I feel a wave of excitement surge through my body, tickling my fingers and toes. My father has invited me to stay. While I am not a member of the council, and anyone is welcome to attend, he invited me to stay. I don't have to rush back to my mother or hear a lecture about remaining silent at a council meeting. I get to listen to them discuss what they will do with the village and hear them consider my suggestion.

"What do we think about building higher?" Terrick asks. "Do we have the skills to do it?" The men continue to mumble to each other. "What would we need to build upward?"

"We haven't done it before," one man says.

"What if the Nadeens attack?" another asks. "How do we know that building taller won't result in more casualties?"

"Who is to say it would?" my father says. "Everyone evacuates to the caves. No one stays in their homes."

"But if they are in their homes when the Nadeens attack, the people are away from the ground. There is a further distance to fall, or escape."

"True." My father points to the map. "If we build further out, there is a greater distance to run to reach the caves. Regardless of what we do, there will be issues we need to consider."

Terrick looks at the map. "If we can't negotiate land, building taller might be a solution. As Colfar said, we could then re-purpose land previously used for homes to build more gardens. It still might not be a long-term solution, but it will keep us going for a few more years."

"The Nadeens won't be interested in negotiating additional land," says the man with the mustache. "The Nadeens made it clear to us before that they want us east, on the opposite side of the Klarish Mountains."

"And those mountains are almost impossible to climb," Terrick says. "Even a healthy person would struggle to make it over. How would we move our children and elderly?"

"Years ago, the Nadeens gave Brocklund Miller permission to construct a village on land over the Klarish Mountains. He broke the agreement with the Nadeens and they're holding to it."

"I can understand why he didn't cross," Hayden says. "If he couldn't get people over the mountains—"

"The Nadeens knew what they were doing when they offered that land to him," the man says. "They were unhappy that he broke away from them and hoped that the people who left with him wouldn't make it over the mountain range. They wanted people to give up and come back. Otherwise, they hoped that if Brocklund Miller crossed over, he wouldn't make it back. When Brocklund saw the range, he knew the people couldn't make it over and built here - on Nadeen land."

"I know people have said it doesn't matter what Brocklund Miller did," Terrick says, "but it impacts our lives now. The Nadeens want us to move our village over the mountains. Brocklund Miller had elderly and young people with him at the time and couldn't make the climb. We still have the same mix of population. We can't ask families to leave their loved ones behind to build a new village there. I'm sure we can expect the community will say either we all move, or we all stay. Given that we know the only place we could move is over the mountains, I believe it is safe to assume we are staying."

"Are you also saying there is no point in negotiating?" the man asks.

"The Nadeens will begin by stating that they want to stick to the original agreement they gave to Brocklund Miller and will deny us expanding," Terrick says.

"But are you still thinking we can attempt a negotiation?"

"I think we should. At least we would know if it were off the table or not. Perhaps, we could also see about a treaty that includes acknowledging the land we already have. What does everyone else think?" Hands rise around the table. "Then we will ask. Who should we nominate to send a radio transmission to the Nadeens?" Terrick asks.

The men turn and face my father, who nods in acknowledgement.

"I will look into sending a transmission this afternoon," my father says. "I will report back when I hear a response."

"That sounds like a plan." Terrick places both hands on the table. "Thank you, Aldon."

"I can investigate what it would take to construct taller buildings," Hayden says. "We might as well keep that moving forward should the Nadeens reject our request."

"That would be good, Hayden," Terrick says. "Unless there is anything else you want to discuss, I will dismiss us for lunch. We will revisit this part of the conversation when we hear from Aldon with news from the Nadeens. Let's eat."

Chairs scrape along the wood-planked floor as the men rise from the table. My father smiles at me and picks up his lunch. "Want to eat with me?" he asks.

"Sure."

He slides his back along the wall and sits on the floor. I lower myself beside him and he breaks apart his roll, handing me half.

"That was a good idea," he says before taking a bite.

"You think so? I didn't know if you would be okay with my speaking up or not since I'm just a kid."

"That was not a problem. We should hear a good idea, and that was an idea we hadn't heard yet."

One by one, the men leave the building. I watch as Terrick nods at me and slips out the door of the meeting hall. Only my father and I remain. I finally get my father to myself, and it isn't because I am in trouble.

"Do you really think it was a good idea?" I ask.

"I do. I wouldn't lie to you." He wraps his arm across my shoulders and pulls me to his side. "I am very proud of you, Colfar."

"Even after all the mistakes I've made?"

"Even after. You are smart and see a vision for our community. Some people don't have the same interest in making improvements as you do. They have lost hope. You see how things can be better, rather than accepting what is. You will make a fine leader one day."

We sit together, sharing portions of my father's lunch, staring out at the empty chairs around the table. One day I could be here as a member of the council, no longer a child observing from the back of the room. I have the support of my father, who feels I could be a leader, like him.

My shoulders roll back as I feel pride welling within me. Not a selfish pride, but a sense of being pleased with who I am now and who I will become. Here, with my father, I am content with the path I am on and my father's approval. If only I could show the other adults that I can be of use now, and not only when I become an adult. I'm ready to do what we need to give my community a chance at a better life. Sharing at the council meeting is a start, but it is not enough.

The men return from their lunch with conversations already in motion. Their voices are loud. Emotions are high. It is as if they never ate but have continued their discussions for the duration of their break.

"Our focus can't be on how we will make room for expansion, but on how we can protect lives," one man says. "We know the Nadeens won't want to negotiate for more land. It is naïve to think they will. The Nadeens feel we are in debt to them. For us to move forward, we need to shift our focus. We need to remove the barrier between us by returning what was theirs."

Hayden sighs. "But we already said we don't have everything that was taken by Brocklund. We can't return what we don't have."

My father refolds what remains of his lunch and rises to his feet, retaking his position at the table. His lunch break is over. Maybe I don't want to be a leader if it means I have to listen to people argue all the time.

"When I begin my conversations with the Nadeens," my father says, "I will find out if they want us to compensate them for the items Brocklund Miller took. In the meantime, we should put an inventory together of what remains of the original supplies and determine if we need replacements or if we have comparable items to provide in exchange." The way my father presents himself to these men leaves me in awe. This is a different man than the one I see at the dinner table every day. At home, he is quiet and soothing. Here, he is strong and in control. If Terrick wasn't in the room, I would guess that my father is the primary leader of the village as the men listen to him, as they do Terrick. The way they keep their eyes fixed on him when he speaks, it is clear he commands their respect. "We will need to talk with the Nadeens about what we can do to make up for lost materials. Our goal should be to negotiate a peace for the land we have now. The next step would be to talk about additional land. There is no point in asking for additional land if they will attack us over what has happened in the past and the land we have."

"We need the equipment for ourselves," a man says. He stares across the table, scowling at my father. "We can't give it back."

"If we can give them equipment in exchange for permanent ownership of our land, it is something we should consider. They might not want to talk to us if we won't consider this," my father says.

"If we give it back, we won't have anything to work the new land. It will impact our capabilities in the blacksmith shops.... all of our trades."

"I understand that, but if there is peace, we will put our energy into creating what we've lost instead of repairing what they destroy," my father says, not backing down.

Terrick walks around the table and stands beside my father. I watch the man across from them take a step back. It is fascinating to watch the men interact. From my perspective, the two most respected men in the room are now standing side-by-side.

"We need to continue to explore the idea, as this is a possibility," Terrick says. "We need an inventory of what was taken by Brocklund and what we can offer as part of our negotiations. Only then can we accurately assess the impact of the offer. The more preparation we can do, the better."

"We could suggest returning items as we can," my father says. "The items we have duplicates of, we could return immediately. Then, take time to return the items with the greatest impact to us, giving us time to replicate them."

"Or see if we can come up with an agreeable form of compensation for keeping it," Hayden says.

The man across the table shakes his head and takes several

steps back. "I say we take what we have and carry it over the Klarish Mountains while we can."

"The equipment is heavy," my father says. "And not everyone would make the journey. We've discussed this. Equipment is not as important as lives."

"Then we only take the people that can make it."

"I can't believe you said that." My father rubs the back of his neck and hangs his head low. "The reason we have this council is to do what is right for the people in the community. Abandoning the weak ones is contrary to everything this council, and all this community stands for. What would happen to the people who can't make it over the mountains? Do we leave them behind to be at the mercy of the Nadeens? I'm talking about our aged and our young families. Little children who wouldn't make it over. You have a grandchild. Are you suggesting we leave her behind?"

The man rubs the side of his cheek and shakes his head. His cheeks sag, and he slips behind the other leaders, turning his face away from my father.

"We can't help everyone," another man shouts, "but we can help the majority."

"We aren't abandoning anyone," Terrick says. "As much as you don't like it, we have no choice but to follow what Aldon has suggested. We negotiate a peace settlement for our existing land. Even if we need to work to give our surplus supplies to pacify the Nadeens, we will figure out something. I can't agree to leaving people behind to suffer at the hands of the Nadeens because we aren't willing to be uncomfortable and give up what was never should have been ours." He takes a breath. "Now, because this is our first contact, we won't be asking for additional land. We will need to look at temporary measures to accommodate the people we have and the food supplies we need to have in place. Colfar came up with what appears to be a workable option. We will look into building vertically. Taller buildings."

The men turn and look at me. Their eyes narrow. I press my back against the wall. I don't want to see the scowls of the men who disagree. Instead, I look at the faces of the men who do. My father, Terrick, Hayden and two other faces of men whose names I can't recall. Their faces are kind.

"I can't believe we're taking direction from a child," a man says.

Terrick turns. "He saw an opportunity we didn't. He deserves credit for it, regardless of his age."

"If he wasn't Aldon's son, I doubt we would have given his suggestion another thought."

"Is that what you think of this council?" Terrick asks, stepping forward. "Do you think we show favoritism toward others because of who they know or how they are related? I'd like to think better of the men in this room. Colfar's idea was a good one, which is why we were talking about it before our break. We don't have the land to build and need more land for food. How can we free up more land in the interim? We build up. Building horizontally is using more space than we have. Vertical solves that problem. None of us, as adults, thought of that solution. Do you really want to disregard his suggestion because you can't see past his age?"

A new lump forms in my throat. I rise to my feet and fight the urge to slip out of the door. It is uncomfortable hearing them fight because of me.

My father glances in my direction and smiles. "Whether or not he is my son," he turns back, "we need to try something, and this gives us more time. We can work on a few designs and test them out. By working on a few vertical homes, we at least will have a clearer understanding if this is a viable option."

"If it's not and the talks fail?" a man asks.

"Then we'll decide what we will do. Who knows, asking them for more land could stir up more trouble than we're prepared for. Climbing over those mountains must be a last resort. I'd rather try this first than choose the option we know will end up in the loss of lives."

The men grumble to each other, and my father gives me a wink. I force a smile in return. Why is he going through all of this trouble for me? I find it hard to believe my idea was that good. I blurted it out and now they are fighting over it. My job was to deliver my father's lunch and then leave. Now, I am helping the adults to decide for the village. I am a contributor. I am finally doing what I have always wanted. I only wish my help didn't come with trouble.

CHAPTER SIX

Over a restless night, I have been thinking about the events of the day before. Coming to mind were the men who disapproved of the option to build vertically or to return the equipment taken so many years ago. What if my idea to build vertically fails? What if they wasted time because of my stupid idea? The men will blame me for it, or if they can't blame a child, they will blame my father.

Many of the men want to either leave the valley altogether, which is impossible, or seek an agreement with the Nadeens to gain more land. But what land? The only land I can picture using is the land I see almost every day from atop of the viewpoint. The land with rolling hills, just above our valley. If the Nadeens were to agree to this, no one would need to travel far to visit each other, and we could all be together. But what if the land is useless? What if it looks luscious and fertile from a distance, but it is only a thin layer of grass growing over hard sandstone?

Someone needs to explore the area and report their findings

to the council. But the councilmen are busy with their own tasks of exploring the option to build vertically and reviewing equipment. Assessing the land is something I could do. It doesn't have to be a thorough report, but it could be a start. I could look for obvious issues. How hard could it be?

In the morning, I quickly finish my chores and search the village to find Rory and Hart to tell them about the events of the day before in the meeting hall and the leadership's plans to execute my idea.

"That's amazing," Rory says.

"It makes me wonder how stupid their own ideas were if they listened to you." I'm not surprised Hart would come back with a backhanded response.

I smile and point to the hills. "Up there is the land we could use. Land that the leadership might build on. They are busy taking an inventory of the equipment, negotiating with the Nadeens, and assessing if we can build taller buildings. None of them talked about exploring the lands to help them decide which land to ask for from the Nadeens. I think we should help."

"By going up there?" Hart asks. "Are you crazy? The leadership has made it clear to everyone that the upper grounds are off limits."

"If we are going to ask for the land, we should at least know if it is any good. We could end up with a useless patch of dirt that is too hard to build or grow on. Something we can't even graze animals on. Why go through the effort and end up with nothing?"

Rory sighs. "Don't you think the adults have thought of that already? Maybe they have other land in mind."

"Perhaps," I say over my shoulder. I'm already on my way,

guiding them towards the overgrown path at the bottom of the valley wall. "If they haven't thought about it yet, we'll have some additional information for them. They'll thank us."

I place my foot on the path and Rory glances behind him. "We'll get in trouble for going up there," he says.

"Maybe, until we tell them what we find," I say, taking another step.

Hart follows me and after briefly hesitating, Rory joins us in climbing the slope up the valley wall.

With the plants growing over the previously worn ground, the trail is hard to make out. Rain has eroded the path, leaving us no choice but to jump over sections of the missing trail. One misstep and we could tumble downward. As we venture up the trail, I glance down at the village. Can the adults see us? Rory was right. If they catch us, we will be in trouble for sure.

My foot slips on the rocky surface, and dirt pours down the valley wall. This entire slope could give way and send soft sand down to the village. I am not surprised that they felt it was too unstable to build homes on. We need to keep moving and not continue to test the stability of the slope.

"Come on, guys," I say to my friends behind me.

They are on my heels. I sense they feel the same about the path.

We continue to guess what is the overgrown path and what is merely where water has worn away any vegetation. We keep going up and that is all the matters at this point. Up will take us to the top of the valley. To get home, we will follow the slope downward. We won't get lost, however, taking the wrong route will increase the difficulty of the journey.

But it is already difficult. My legs ache as I lean closer to the slope. Another step and I dig my fingers into the dirt to claw my way up. Halfway up, it is almost an impossible climb and makes me question how strong I am. Looking at the slope from the village, it didn't appear intimidating or strenuous. Now, I am struggling to make it to the top. This is nothing like the trail that leads to the viewpoint.

Another glance over my shoulder and I see people in the village moving from shop to shop. They have no time to notice three boys climbing the valley wall. If I turn around now, they may never know we left or ventured where they told us not to. My father would never know I have disobeyed him yet again.

I am certain if we were to stop now, we would never be the ones to discover what is up there. The council and the community could end up relying on what someone has told them in the past instead of exploring and gathering fresh information. This will give us knowledge. This will help us decide. There must be a place we can go besides remaining confined between the walls of the village.

"We should turn back," Hart says, pointing behind us. "All of this work isn't worth it."

He would say that. Hart hates work and is always complaining about something.

"We're almost to the top," I say, for his benefit and mine. We're not stopping. It is too late to turn around now.

Rory huffs and puffs behind me. "Don't give up, Hart. You can do it."

Hart is strong enough to make it, but until we reach the top, we will have to listen to his complaints. I was half expecting this reaction from him. Anything we do, besides playing Tusselball, earns negative comments from him. In fact, I had considered not inviting him to come along with us. I had no choice but to include him or I would have to listen to him complain later about being excluded.

"This was a stupid idea," Hart says.

"No, it's not," I say. "You're just saying that because you're tired."

"And hot."

It is hot. The dirt sticks to my sweat-covered skin as the sun beats down on the back of my neck. If I had prepared better, I would have brought water with me. I will drink when I get home.

"What are you hoping to find up there?" Rory asks.

I have no answer, as there is nothing specific I am looking for. It is knowledge I'm after. To discover if we can use the land? See if there are any dangers.

"I want to know," I say.

"So, we're going through all of this trouble because you're curious?" Hart asks and sighs.

"That is what it sounds like," Rory says, grabbing a rock on the path to pull himself up the hill.

I don't want to push them to go through all of this climbing if they don't see a point in it. I see the point. Knowledge will help the council. It can bring hope to the people in the village. This is a good thing.

"Do you really want to spend the rest of your life living down there?" I pause on a flat patch of dirt. "If this doesn't work, I heard the council talking about moving over the Klarish Mountains."

"No way," Hart says. His fingers grip a stone to hold him steady.

We have never ventured close to the mountains before, but we have all heard stories about them.

"Didn't someone die trying to climb over them?" Rory asks.

"That's what I heard," Hart says. "And from what they described, I imagine the climb is even worse than this one. I would die trying to climb the Klarish Mountains."

Rory laughs. "Are you going to die on this trip?"

"I might. I don't think it will be a fall that kills me."

Resuming our climb up the slope, I understand why the council is hesitant to move our village over the mountains. This slope is relatively short and not nearly as steep as the mountains would be. If three kids our age are tired, those younger than us or the elderly would never make it over. But what if they could make this short climb with help? What if we agree with the Nadeens and they allow us to live here? We could construct something that could make this climb easier for those in the community if they lived on the upper grounds.

After a few more steps, my foot touches the top of the slope. In front of me, the land is green with rolling hills. This land is perfect for grazing animals. If we continue to explore, we may find an ideal place to build a second village. Already, my heart is racing. This is what I have dreamed it would be, and I am standing on it.

"Smell that grass," I say, stepping further away from the slope.

"We should head back," Rory says. "Now that we've seen what's up here, we should get back before they notice we're gone. We don't want to get into any more trouble than we will be in already."

"No one knows we're here," I say. I run my hand over the blades of grass and press my hand into the soil.

"They'll find out."

Hart sighs. "After climbing that hill, I'm not ready to go back down just yet. I have earned a little time up here. I want to rest first."

For once, Hart's complaining is helpful. I want to see more of the area and Hart doesn't want to climb back down. I will get more time up here.

A wind blows and the grass blades rub together, creating a rattling noise. I have never heard a field of grass like this before. In the village valley, we have odd prickly shrubs that decorate the ground, and the branches of trees create their own creaking noise in the wind, but expansive open fields are something we don't have between the valley walls.

Already, I am delighted by what I've found. I pluck a blade from the ground. It is soft and bends between my fingers. I lift it to my nose and let its scent fill my nostrils. I drop to the ground where I lie on my back, letting my arms swim in the green grass. It is cool and soft against my exposed skin. I had expected the blades to poke and scratch me, but they are smooth and feel like a bed.

"Colfar," Rory says, standing over me. "What are you doing?"

"Lie down on it."

"Why? It's just grass."

"It's not like our grass. This stuff is soft."

After taking a moment to consider my suggestion, Rory and Hart are beside me on the grass, staring up at the clear sky.

"Isn't this nice?" I ask.

"The grass is cold," Hart says with a whine.

I sigh. "It's not that cold, Hart. Why don't you relax and enjoy yourself?"

Hart drapes his arm over his eyes. "It's too bright, too."

"Is there anything else you don't like about this place?" I ask.

"It's too open. There's no place to hide."

I shake my head. How could anyone feel the need to hide here? It is beautiful. I feel calm. I feel at home. "What do you need to hide from?"

"The Nadeens," he says.

The Nadeens have a way of ruining everything. Hart can't even enjoy a moment of lying on soft grass without thinking about what the Nadeens might do.

"They aren't here," I say.

"Not yet, but they could be watching us," Hart says. There is a weight of fear in his voice. "They told us not to be up here, remember? This is their land."

"The Nadeens think they own all of Elta. Even where we live now, they claim is theirs," I say. "What does it matter if we are up here or down there?"

"At least they let us live there instead of forcing us over the mountains," Rory says.

"They let us live there?" I laugh. "We're just sitting in the valley, waiting for them to attack again."

I know I'm not the only one who thinks this way. I've heard my parents and the council talk about it. They believe that with no formal agreement in place, the Nadeens will continue to attack. Even though what happened between us and the Nadeens occurred before my father or Terrick were born, the Nadeens still view us as squatters. To them, we are pests who left their city and built a village on land that belongs to them. But where else were we supposed to go?

"If they will attack us regardless of where we live," I say, "don't you think we should at least flourish and spread out to places where we can grow food and graze our animals? Building here, we would have more room. Not being in a small space, it would be harder for them to destroy everything. Maybe people's attitudes would change, too, if we weren't living in such a cramped valley. People get grumpy when they feel trapped."

"You're talking about Marlow," Rory says.

"Exactly. He could have his patch of grass and I could have mine. There would be no reason for him to fight with me anymore."

"Or for you to fight with him," Rory tucks his arm behind his head. "Colfar, you aren't perfect."

"Marlow asks for it."

"And so, do you. After that fight the other day, I had several adults ask me about what happened. I don't enjoy being questioned or involved in your stuff."

"Then just tell them you know nothing."

"That's what I did. They know you tell me everything and I'm not good at keeping secrets like you."

I sit up and pivot on the grass toward him. "What did you tell them?"

"Only that the two of you have been having issues with each other for a while. I mentioned that you told me how Marlow said a few words and you… well, you fought him."

"I didn't want to fight him."

"You did. Why else did you jump at the chance?" Rory sits up beside me.

"I fought him because he had been kicking me and said my parents might die."

"Anyone could die. And they will one day. Hopefully, not until they're old."

"But he makes comments all the time." I can't believe my friend isn't backing me up on this.

"You make comments to him, Colfar. He's lost his parents. He's a little sensitive."

"He shouldn't be," I say. Rory blinks and his mouth hangs open. In this moment, I remember what I forgot. Rory knows what it feels like to lose a parent. In my wish to defend myself, I have unintentionally hurt my friend. Someone who has lost his father.

"I'm sorry, Rory."

"Don't say anything," he says, raising his hand. "You have no right to say someone shouldn't be sensitive about the death of their family."

"That's not what I was trying to say."

"What were you trying to say? Think before you answer."

I didn't mean to offend my friend. If by suggesting someone shouldn't be sensitive was offensive, I need to make it right. Rory can't think I don't care that he has lost his father. "I was wrong. I shouldn't say anything about his parents. But I don't want to hear someone say he hopes my parents will die."

"He's not saying that. At least, I hope he isn't. What did he tell you?"

"That I could be in his shoes one day."

"And...?"

"That's it. That's the same as saying my parents will die."

"It isn't the same," Rory says.

"Sure, it is. By saying I could be like him—"

"Deep down, he's saying he wants no one to feel the same loss he does. Even you, Colfar. He wants nothing to happen to your parents. He's asking you to think because one day, you could be in the same position as him and someone could say the same words to you. Every time someone talks about my father, it hurts. It's a reminder he's gone."

Rory is saying that Marlow cares and doesn't wish ill-will on me or my parents? Hard to believe. However, if I have to trust someone on this, it will be Rory.

Hart springs to his feet. "Did you hear that?"

"Hear what?" I ask, looking up at the empty sky.

"In the grass." He points toward the ground, a few feet from where he had been resting. "Something is moving."

I watch the grass. The wind still bends the blades as it blows through. "All the grass is moving. It's the wind."

"It wasn't the wind. This was different."

Rory and I sit in silence, while Hart watches the wind blow the grass back and forth.

"There." He points a little further out, where the grass is bending differently than the blades in the wind. A few feet away, the grass parts like something is moving away from us. Hart takes a step forward.

Rory and I rise from the ground and follow Hart, who is now only a foot from the parting grass.

He takes another step forward. A long, black snake leaps toward him and he falls backward, kicking his feet recklessly in the air. The grass parts again, but now is parting toward Hart. Returning to his feet, he takes several steps back. The snake hisses and springs forward again, soaring above the grass and landing inches from Hart's toes.

I look around for something to throw or beat back the snake. There is nothing.

"Run," I shout.

And we do.

The snake nips at Hart's heels until he has left the snake far enough in the distance and he is no longer a threat to it, or the snake a threat to Hart.

He pants, catching his breath. Rory and I do the same. I bend forward, looking at the surrounding grass, checking for any other snakes nearby.

"That was close," Rory says, holding his hand to his chest. "That Raven Snake didn't bite you, right?"

Hart looks down at his legs. "No. I would be dead if it did."

"True."

It is common to hear of someone dying every year from a Raven Snake bite. We have no cure and their victims die in a matter of hours. Had it bitten Hart, he would already feel the pain searing through his veins. He is lucky. We all are.

"Can we go back now?" Hart asks, placing his hands to his knees. His face is pale. "That has done me in."

"Me, too," Rory says.

I turn toward the unexplored rolling hills. It is too soon to turn back. There is still so much we don't know. Even after that fright, I don't want to go home, yet. "You guys can go back."

"Colfar." Rory steps toward me. "We can't go back without you."

"Why not? It's just down the hill."

"Your parents wouldn't forgive us if something happened to you up here, and we left you."

"Nothing will happen."

Hart laughs. "Seconds ago, a Raven Snake chased me through the grass, and you want us to leave you up here so you can become its next meal?"

"I won't get bit. If you want to go back, then go. I'll be fine."

They look at each other and shrug their shoulders.

"Promise me you won't stay up here long," Rory says.

"I won't. I only want to see what is by the hills." When I get over there, I may also want to see what is over the hills and beyond, but they needn't know that. They can go back. I will continue to explore and see if there is anything else I can find that might help our village.

Rory and Hart walk back to the slope and I stand in the field, looking out at my new surroundings. It is open and bright. The only shadows cast down on the field are from the light, puffy clouds above. Here, the possibilities for our village are endless. One day we could plant a grove of fruit trees and a garden for more vegetables. The openness could support the construction of more homes. This land looks rich and fertile. It is usable land and has been sitting right above our heads this entire time.

CHAPTER SEVEN

In the distance, low hills change the appearance of an otherwise flat landscape and I make my way toward them. The grass rubs against my legs, tickling my skin, and the sun shines down on me as I cross the field leading to the base of the hills. It is as if the sun has welcomed me up here. The breeze cools my skin and I briefly close my eyes. Finally, I am not limited to where I can go. I feel free.

It would be great if our community could experience this land for themselves. Having walked up here, the lower valley will now feel like a confined pit. Believing years of stories has kept people from leaving the village and exploring this space, keeping them trapped down in the valley. If only the others were brave enough to climb the slope, then they could see this place for themselves.

Alone, I walk through the grass field toward the hills, keeping watch for another snake. Every rattle of grass blades blowing in the wind makes me jump. If I am bitten, it will be the end of me, but it will surprise me if I run into another Raven Snake. They are territorial and won't allow another snake onto their turf. Still, I tread lightly and watch where I place my feet.

Ahead, the grass thins, making more rocks and sand visible at the base of the hills. Large boulders and smaller rocks lie in clusters. From the viewpoint, the hills had looked connected, rolling from one hill to the next. Now, I see they are individual hills. Rows and rows of small to medium-sized hills. Short green and yellow grasses grow on the hills' tiered surface, formed by years of erosion. While I can't picture us building homes on these hills, I wonder how we could use them? Raised gardens, perhaps? Maybe animals could walk up them while grazing?

I move between the first row of hills. Never has this much green grass surrounded me, or have I had it rise above me in pillows of green. I navigate a narrow grassy path between the hills. The slopes are like walls as I walk between them. I want to climb the mounds. There could be another magnificent view on the other side.

A taller hill stands at a fork in the path, and I make my way toward it. This hill will give me the best view. Like the hills before, at its base are more clusters of gray boulders and rocks. It makes me believe water once flowed through these hills and jammed them together until this became their ultimate resting place.

I look up at the giant hill and take a breath. I must climb and see what lies beyond. With one foot on the grass, I lean into the hill. Sand slides under my feet, weaving between the blades of grass. If this is the condition of the soil, it may rule out gardening.

"You are a long way from home," I hear a voice say behind me.

I turn.

A boy sits at the top of the boulder among the cluster of rocks at the base of the hill. He has trimmed his hair short and while his clothes are crisp, a layer of mud covers them. The boy folds his arms across his chest as he stares me down. Judging by his size, he is about the same age as me.

My heart pounds in my chest. He is not one of us.

"Who are you?" I ask, stepping off the hill.

"Does it matter?" The boy leans back on his elbows, making it harder to see him.

I strain to get a better look at him, rising to the tips of my toes. "Where are you from?" I ask, as I take a step toward him. "Are you a Nadeen?"

He tilts his head to the side and straightens his back. "What do you think?" He fixes his eyes on me.

I take another step forward. "I think you are."

"Stay back," he shouts, rising to his feet. "If you come any closer, I will have to hurt you."

I have only just met him, and he is already threatening violence. There is no question, he is a Nadeen. "I won't come closer. I won't hurt you." I hold my position and stare back at the boy on the rocks. If he has walked here, he has traveled far.

I stare at him as I feel my legs shake. My heart continues to beat against my chest. I am face-to-face with a Nadeen. I imagine he must feel the same anxiety as I do, and that may be why he threatened to hurt me. He has probably never been this close to one of us before. Given the stories they have told him about my people, I need to show him a good first impression and prove the stories are wrong.

"My name is Colfar," I say. He says nothing. I try my best to form a warm smile. If my father is trying to negotiate for more land, I will need to appear friendly and maybe get this boy on our side. "I've come from the village down the hill."

He nods his head. "I already determined that. Why are you out here, Colfar?"

"Exploring."

I wait for him to respond. "Do you explore up here often?"

"No. This is my first time." I look over my shoulder, toward the village. "I could get into a lot of trouble for being up here."

"Why is that?" he asks. His muscles relax, and he resumes his previous lean against the boulder.

"Because no one is allowed to be up here. We're supposed to stay down in the valley. I didn't get permission to be up here, and they wouldn't have given it if I asked."

He nods, but his face is otherwise expressionless, giving me no sign of what he is thinking.

"Why are you here?" I ask the boy. If I keep him talking, I might learn more about him.

His head tilts. "Exploring… like you. However, I am here because I am permitted to be."

"Near the village?"

He nods again. "I can go where I want."

"That must be nice," I say. He has the freedom to explore all areas of Elta. There are no restrictions when you are a Nadeen… unless you are a Nadeen wanting to explore our village. The council would never allow him between the valley walls.

"How far have you traveled?" I ask, looking again at his muddy clothes.

"That is none of your business," he snaps back.

"Why?"

He slides his legs over the edge of the boulder and climbs off the rock. With one last jump, he plants his feet on the ground. A plume of dust lifts around his previously polished shoes. "Because this is our land. You are the one who is away from home. As long as I am on our land, I am home."

I fight the urge to respond. Allowing myself to respond to taunts has only ever led to trouble with Marlow. But he need not remind me that all of Elta's land belongs to the Nadeens. Even though he has the freedom to go where he wants, the Nadeens' city is a multi-day hike from here. He has no business being so far from where he lives.

"Shouldn't you be closer to the city?" I ask. "Someone your age shouldn't roam so far away from adults." I cross my arms.

"You as well. Exploring land that belongs to the Nadeens is unwise," he says. He moves closer and I take a step back. "You said you would be in trouble if the adults found out you are up here. So, I can assume that no one knows you are here." He continues to draw closer, and I step further away. "What do you think will happen when I return home and tell our leaders there was a Miller boy walking around the hills?"

A Miller boy. That's all I am to him. He is a Nadeen, and I am a Miller. Why did the adults have to teach him that we are different? I am only a person who wants for our people to live peacefully. What happened years ago between their leadership and Brocklund Miller when he left is not my fault.

Even after years of war and hearing stories about the

Nadeens, I don't want to kill them, or this boy. I want to live peacefully and for my family and other families to be safe. He needs to see that I am no threat. Maybe this meeting could become the start of peace between our people. I have to try.

I clear my throat. "You could tell them we met and talked."

He laughs. "Why would I share that? You have said nothing that interests me, or them."

"Not yet, but I might."

"That is if I intend to keep talking to you."

"Who else are you going to talk to, if not me? There's no one else here."

His head tilts again and his hand drifts up to the side of his head. "You are right. There is no one else." He tugs on the collar of his shirt and lifts his chin. "So, Colfar, what have you found during your exploration?" A lighter tone. Maybe my plan is working?

"I have found these hills," I say, holding my arms out wide. "I found a Raven Snake earlier. Well, my friend found it."

He pauses and looks past me. "Where is your friend now?"

"He and my other friend returned to the village. The snake scared them off."

"And you stayed up here on your own?"

"I wasn't ready to go back, yet. I've always looked out at these fields, wishing I could walk in them. This might be my only chance to be up here, so I wanted to stay and keep looking."

"For what?" he asks.

"I don't know. I wanted to see… See if it was possible to live up here."

He straightens his back. "You are lying."

"I'm not."

"You are. They sent you up here. The adults." He backs up toward the boulder. "They think a child would never be in trouble if he wandered away from the village."

"No. I'm telling the truth," I say, taking a step forward. He takes another step back. With my heart racing and the sound of its beating ringing in my ears, I had forgotten about his original request for me to stay back. I freeze in place. "Like you said, the adults don't know I'm up here. They didn't send me."

"They have to know. Miller children are always supervised."

"We aren't always supervised…" I turn toward the village and then back to the boy standing in front of the boulders. "Are you being supervised?"

He stares at me. His hand drifts toward his ear and then back to his side. "No. I am not. You ask a lot of questions for someone who has wandered away from home. Children, like you, can be dangerous." He takes another step toward me and I am now standing only a few feet away from a Nadeen.

"Not all children," I say, holding my ground. I've been through enough situations like this with Marlow. He won't intimidate me, and I won't run away.

A smile crosses his lips. "So, you are not as scared as you first appeared."

I swallow away a lump in my throat. I don't want to get into a fight with a Nadeen. I want the opposite. I want peace, but don't want him to think I'm weak. "You don't scare me," I say.

He laughs again. "If I do not scare you, why do you keep walking backwards when I approach you?"

"I am giving you space. This is your land."

"It is." He taps his foot on the ground and crosses his arms across his chest. "Do you plan to keep talking to me?"

"Yes."

"Why?"

"Because I want to make sure my people are safe."

He sighs and lowers his arms to his side. "Do you see any aircraft?"

"No."

"Then you are your people are safe." He backs toward the boulder and places his hand on the rock. "We are done here."

"Wait." I take another few steps toward him and he removes his hand from the boulder to hold it out in front of him, reminding me to stay back. I do. This could be my only chance to get this boy to trust me. If we keep talking, maybe I could show my desire for peace, or if he has left the Nadeens, we could take in a tired, hungry, and scared boy. "Are you staying up here long?" I ask. "Can I bring you anything?"

"No," he says.

"Food? Are you hungry?"

"Maybe food. Are you saying you will come back tomorrow?"

"If you will be here, yes. It's the least I can do."

"Then I will see you tomorrow," he says. "And don't tell the adults we met, or you will be in trouble."

In trouble with my father, or with the Nadeens?

At the base of the slope, I am hidden behind a home where I huddle between Rory and Hart to recount what I found at the hills. I tell them about the boy. A Nadeen who has wandered away from home. Their eyes widen and they fidget in place.

"I'm taking food to him tomorrow," I say.

"You're what? Why would you bring food to a Nadeen?" Rory asks. He looks around the corner of the home. There are no adults nearby. No one can hear us.

"What if he tries to kill you?" Hart leans against the building's wall and frowns. "This has got to be one of the stupidest things you have ever done, Colfar."

"He won't try to kill me." I give him my best reassuring smile. "I'm sure it scared him to be talking to me, too."

"If it scared him," Hart says, "then he is probably long gone. He has no reason to stick around here, and risk being found."

"Exactly," Rory whispers. "It would scare me if I was near the Nadeens' city and ran into someone like him. How would I know someone wouldn't come back and try to kill me?"

"I told him I wouldn't hurt him," I say.

Hart laughs. "As if that means anything."

"Hey. I would never—"

"I didn't mean you," Hart says, taking a step back. "I know you wouldn't have hurt him. If a Nadeen was to say the same thing, I wouldn't believe them. Why should the boy believe you?"

"You have a point." The boy has no reason to trust me. He even threatened me. But if I don't follow through and bring him food, I would be a liar. I had every intention of bringing him food when I made that promise. To earn his trust, I need to do what I said I would. "I will meet him again tomorrow. He's up there all alone and probably needs someone to talk to. Maybe, he has left the city for good. I could convince him to come down and stay with us. What if he meets with the leadership and tells them what is happening at the Nadeens' city? He could be helpful."

Rory takes a step toward me. "Colfar, I think you need to talk to the council about this. If not them, then at least your father."

I shake my head. "I don't want to risk scaring the boy off."

"You don't have to tell him you talked to your father, but you shouldn't be talking to Nadeens on your own."

I shake my head again and move away. "You don't trust me."

Rory looks over his shoulder and turns back. "I trust you," he says. "I don't trust the Nadeens."

"He's only a boy."

"And so are you," Rory says. "What makes you think you can do this without at least talking to the adults about it?"

"I will… eventually. Just not yet." I can't believe he would suggest I am stupid enough to exclude the council, or my father. I'm not looking to be a hero. I am only trying to help and this kid could have answers. We'll only be able to get those answers if we talk to him. If I bring the adults into it now, who knows how they'd react. They could say I can't talk to him at all. Then what? He could run off and refuse to talk to any of us again. What good would that do? I don't want to miss this opportunity.

"You need to tell them soon," Rory says.

"Why is that?"

"Because, if you don't… I will."

"You wouldn't." I stare at my friend and fight a desire to wrestle him to the ground. How dare he threaten to talk to the adults? He could ruin everything when I am trying to help the council bring peace to Elta.

Hart steps forward. “I agree with Rory,” he says. “You’re being stupid.”

“Why did I even tell you two?”

“Telling us was the right thing to do,” Rory says. “It would be even better if you told someone older than us.”

“I’m done with this,” I say. “If you don't like it, stay out of it. I will tell them myself.” I turn away. What is the point in talking to them anymore? I agree that the adults should know, but I don’t need Rory and Hart telling me when I should tell them. There is a boy up there who needs me, and I will do what I have to get him to trust me. I don’t need a lecture from people who are supposed to be my friends.

CHAPTER EIGHT

"I have been in contact with the Nadeens." My father's cooling dinner sits on his plate in front of him. He hasn't taken a single bite.

My mother's back straightens. "And?" Her fork slides across the surface of her plate.

"They put me in touch with a young man named Tarsen. He and I had a lengthy conversation today."

My father has also been talking to the Nadeens. We have something in common. If only we could talk about the boy in the hills. We could talk about our successful conversations. But that would distract him from his work. His job of negotiating is important. Telling him about the boy might redirect his focus. By talking to the boy and convincing him I am trustworthy, word could get back to the Nadeens and convince the adults that my father is also trustworthy.

"And what did this Tarsen, say?" my mother asks.

I lean forward, and my father gives me a slight smile. He

must see I am eager to hear another one of his stories, only he doesn't know the true reason for my increased interest.

"Well," my father says, "Tarsen was as cold as I know the Nadeens to be. I don't like how formal they all are in how they speak. They are an uptight bunch."

My mother pushes her plate forward. "Aside from that, did he say they will entertain our request for more land?"

My father lets out a laugh. "The Nadeens know who has the upper hand. They are only interested in negotiating us off the land we already have. Tarsen said they will assure us safe passage over the mountains and won't attack from behind if we leave quietly."

I hear a gasp from my mother, who covers her mouth. "They didn't," she says.

"Oh, they did. Tarsen instructed us to pack up the entire village and move east, claiming there is plenty of land there, waiting for us."

After hearing the council talk about the logistics of moving east, over the Klarish Mountains, I know this won't be an option. The offer of land to the east means nothing if we can't reach it.

"What would keep them from flying over the mountains with their aircraft to attack us again?" my mother asks. "The Nadeens have said they own all of Elta. Why not claim the east side of the mountains, too?"

My father laughs again. "I believe they feel we wouldn't survive the trip. There would be no one alive to attack."

My mother looks down at the table. I can see the lines of tension on her face. She is concerned, and that makes me concerned. "So, we either die where we are," she says, "or we die trying to climb over the mountains, is that it?"

"That's exactly it," my father says.

My mother looks over at me, and I quickly focus my eyes on my plate. "We shouldn't be talking about these types of things in front of Colfar."

"You can talk in front of me," I say. "I don't mind. What does Tarsen sound like, Father? Did he sound old?"

"Young. Tough. He wasn't that interested in negotiating at first, but after a while, he said he would take our request back to the council. Their first offer of having us move over the mountains might not be a final one."

I feel a little excited by the news that Tarsen was at least willing to think about it. My plan to use my interactions with the boy to help negotiations might be of use, especially if the Nadeens haven't finalized their decision. I still have time to build trust with him. "Do you think Tarsen will come back with an answer soon? Did he say how long you will have to wait?"

"I have scheduled another conversation with him tomorrow. He said he would have a response for us then."

I have less time than I hoped.

My mother rises from the table and clears away her dish. "Tonight, will feel like a long evening then. I hate waiting for responses from anyone. With all of this talk about treaties and land negotiations…" She sighs. "We can't move forward with anything until they say something."

"I am not holding my breath," my father says. "I fully expect them to come back with a rejection. In fact, the council is talking about being on alert. Since we have never made a request like this before, it concerns us that the Nadeens may lash out."

"What kind of way?" she asks, returning to the table. "Are you thinking they might attack?"

"It's possible. They may want to shut down this kind of talk early and push us toward moving away from the valley. Terrick and I feel the village needs to consider ways we can better defend ourselves. I wish we could figure out how to bring down the Nadeens' aircraft. Our weapons just aren't strong enough to penetrate the metal exterior on those things."

"I could throw rocks at them," I say.

My father's laugh fills the room. "You'd have to throw some pretty large rocks to even come close to denting them. They wouldn't even hear your pebbles striking them."

I wasn't being serious, but at least it brought a little laughter to the room. The conversation around the table has been too serious and I don't like it. The council is prepared for retaliation from the Nadeens, but I might be able to prevent it. Maybe I can get the boy to come down into the village and talk to the council? Then, we could get him to pass a message to Tarsen and tell the Nadeens we are good people. I promised to bring him food tomorrow. I will ask him to help us and hopefully, he will agree.

With a wrapped bundle of bread in my hands and a quick glance over my shoulder, I take the first few steps up the slope. My legs still burn from the strain of making this climb yesterday, but I push through the aches. There is no time for a break, or for resting my body. Instead, I will let the adrenaline carry me up the hill.

This is an enormous opportunity. I have never heard of a child coming near the village before. There have been rumors of adults scouting the area, but their intentions were never good. It was always to spy. But a child? A lost child? All he needs is for someone to make him feel at home. If the Nadeens see how well we will treat him, they will thank us for taking in one of their own. This could be the start of peace. This could be what we have hoped for.

But only if the boy is still there today. I might have scared him off. Sleeping alone in the hills he had all night to think about our meeting yesterday. He could have convinced himself that I was a threat. I hope he hasn't left.

Watching for snakes, I inch my way over to the boulders at the bottom of the hill. The sunlight casts a shadow at their base. This was where I found him, but I can't see him.

"Are you there?" I call over to the boulder. I take a step forward and glance toward the hills, looking for any sign that he is nearby. "Boy. Are you there?" I call again.

Rocks grind against the ground behind the boulder and dirt slides down its sides. He shows his head above the rock.

"Hello, Colfar," he says. He looks past me, toward the village and around the field. "Are you alone?"

"I am. I didn't think you'd want me to bring a bunch of people along."

He nods.

"I brought you some food," I say, holding out the bundle.

He sits on top of the boulder and reaches his hand toward me. Standing on my toes, I close the gap between us. I stretch upward and he grabs the package from me.

"My mother made it," I say, hoping for a response. "Bread rolls and meat. Try it."

"I will later. I caught a rodent earlier and roasted him up."

I've had my share of roasted rodent, but it has been months since I have experienced the bitter meat. I gag at the memory. This boy will appreciate the meal I have given him. He'll never want to eat rodent meat again.

Relieved at the sight of him sitting on top of the boulder, I exhale. My plan is coming together. I had hoped he would climb down from the boulder to take the package from me, but he sits alone, picking at his teeth with a blade of grass. He takes little notice of me. Kicking at the ground, I wonder what to say next.

I say nothing.

He is the first to speak.

"I had guessed that you changed your mind, so I found something else to eat," he says, coldly.

"I'm sorry I took so long," I say. "I had chores to do."

"Chores?" He laughs and tosses the blade of grass over the edge of the boulder. "Is that all the children in your village do?"

"No. Sometimes we play."

He scratches his head. "You do what?"

"We play." I lower myself to the ground and sit on a dried bed of weeds and stones below the boulder. "We chase balls and run around. Fun stuff like that. Once we finish our chores, we can do what we like."

The boy sighs and rubs his ear. "Do you do anything useful?"

"What do you mean?" Helping with chores is useful.

"Do you train?"

"Train for what?"

"To fight."

"Fight? No." I laugh and as quickly as my laughter begins, I stop. He is scowling at me. Hopefully, my error doesn't damage my relationship with him. "We don't learn to fight. We're kids."

"I know how to fight," he says, lifting his chin. "I know a lot of things. I have been through years of training."

Is he trying to prove something? I can't imagine going through years of training to learn how to fight. I have watched adults practice with their rifles, but never have they offered to teach me how to use one. Is that wrong? "The adults in the village believe that kids don't belong in the war. We don't go through training. When the Nadeens attack, the children hide."

The boy laughs. "The children hide like cowards?"

A heat burns within me. I am not a coward. "I do as I am told. We stay out of the way."

"Because the children in your village are useless."

"We aren't useless. We help."

"Ah. But you told me you do nothing but hide."

"I didn't say that. I said we don't train. We do chores like chop firewood and deliver supplies to people who need them. We don't fire weapons or anything like that."

He shakes his head and leans back on the boulder. "I stand by what I said. The children in your village are useless."

If this was Marlow, we would already be exchanging blows and I would have him pinned to the ground. One of us would be bleeding. But this is a Nadeen. I can't tackle him without ruining the work my father is doing. Besides, they have trained this boy to fight, and I have only fought with Marlow. Who knows what this boy is capable of?

I take a breath and exhale slowly. As the air leaves my body, the tension releases and the urge to fight him eases.

"You had better hope we never fight each other," he says with a smile. "It would be too easy to kill you."

After bringing him food, he is threatening me. Fear is a

strange thing. Despite his words, I need to stick to my plan and do what I can to help my father. "Maybe there will be peace between our people before that happens," I say. A little optimism can't hurt our conversation.

He scratches his head, and the smile disappears from his face. "Why would there be peace? Your people hate us."

I shake my head. "We don't. We want to live in peace. We don't want to fight. It is what I have heard the adults say over and over. No one wants to fight. They want to organize a peace agreement between our people."

"You are lying," he says.

"I'm not. I have seen what happens when your people attack. I don't want to keep seeing others get hurt or killed. Kids don't have their parents anymore because of the war."

"I have no reason to believe you."

"I can prove it."

He leans back. "Prove it? How?"

"Come to the village and I can introduce you to the leaders. Talk to them and hear for yourself that we want peace."

He is laughing again, and I'm not sure why. "You want me to go to your village and talk to your leaders? What a ridiculous idea. I will not walk into an enemy's village to be captured, tortured, and probably killed. I would be stupid to listen to you. A child who probably has no access to the leaders in your village at all."

"You're wrong. My father is one of them. You could meet him first, and then he could introduce you to the others."

The boy blinks and stares at me. Slowly, his eyebrows rise. "Your father is a leader in your village?"

"Yes. He is."

"Is he a powerful man?"

Now I am laughing as I shake my head. "I wouldn't say that. He does his best to get his point across and is good at persuading people. No one has too much power. Everyone makes their own decisions. It's not just on one person."

The boy shrugs. "Too many decisions help no one. Do you have a key leader? A decision maker?"

I pause for a moment, thinking back to the meeting hall and the men gathered around the table. There has always been one man who has stood out.

"If we did, it would be Terrick."

"Would Terrick let me stay?" he asks. His tone isn't as cold. It has weakened. He sounds more like a child.

"I would think so. If the others agree."

"Does he have a lot of influence?"

"He does, but only because he listens and gives excellent advice. Terrick cares about the people in the village and we know it."

"How many leaders are there? How many would have to agree?"

"There are about eight," I say, recalling the faces in the meeting hall. "There is a core of about four and then they bring others in to the meeting hall to talk about different things, such as food, construction, and supplies. They are good men to talk to."

All color has drained away from the boy's face. After being quick to respond, he is now quiet and nods slowly.

"I'm sure I could get my father to meet you," I say. "If you'd like to meet him."

"I will need to think about it," he says. "How often do your leaders meet?"

"Every few days."

The boy rubs his ear and nods. Taking a breath, he tilts his head to the side and squints his eyes. "Where?" he asks. "Would I have to walk far?"

I smile. I'm getting somewhere. "At the meeting hall. It's near the center of the village. The area isn't that big, so it's a short walk."

"How long do they meet? If I choose to talk to them, would I have to decide in the morning to see them during their meeting?"

The boy is considering it. My cheeks ache as I smile. It is working. "They meet long enough to discuss what needs to get done," I say, feeling out of breath as I rush to answer his question. If answering keeps him from changing his mind, I must answer quickly to make this meeting happen. "I'm sure they would meet with you, even if you talked after their meeting was over. They might arrange a meeting just for you."

He looks toward the village. "What are they talking about now?"

I think back to my father's comments at the dinner table and the Nadeen named Tarsen. I wonder if this boy knows him. "They could be. If so, they are probably talking about the conversations my father has been having with the Nadeens."

"What conversations?" he asks.

"We are negotiating for land. We need more space, and an agreement will allow us to live in peace, while giving us room to grow."

"Grow?" The boy slides back on the boulder. "You have

plenty of space down there and the land you are living on is ours. You want more?"

My heart pounds in my chest. "We need more land to grow food. We aren't trying to take more from you."

"It sure sounds that way."

"I'm sorry. I didn't mean for it to—"

"I am done here," the boy says, climbing down from the boulder.

"Wait," I say. The boy takes a step toward the hills and stops. "Come back tomorrow," I tell him. "Maybe we could continue to talk."

"About what? More things you intend to steal from us? You are all like Brocklund Miller. He stole from us to build that village of yours."

"We're not. Please, come back. I want to get to know you. Maybe we can become friends."

His eyes narrow. "You want to be friends?"

"I do. Will you come back?"

"Only if you bring more food." He turns and walks toward the hills, leaving me fearful that my plan might not work.

CHAPTER NINE

I slide down the final few feet of the slope and land back in the village, hidden behind the same row of shops and homes where I had talked to Hart and Rory. Brushing the dirt from my pants, I search my clothes for any remaining evidence of my adventure above. The adults must never know I was up there until I am ready to tell them.

I exhale.

This was the right time of the day to explore. Everyone has been busy with their daily chores with no time to notice I was away. Given how late in the morning it is, I need to head home and find my mother. She will want me to make deliveries soon. If I am late, she will question where I have been and—

"Colfar," I hear over my shoulder. I freeze. My face cools and my legs shake as knots twist in my stomach. My father is approaching with Terrick and two other men. "What were you doing up here?" my father shouts. His face is red as he points up the slope.

I want to take a step back, but my wobbling legs won't budge. "How did you—"

"Rory and Hart told us," he says, grabbing my elbow.

Just as they had threatened, my friends have betrayed me by telling my father. I told them I would tell my father on my own time. They have meddled with my plans. Who knows what will happen, not only to me, but to my efforts to bring the boy and the leaders together?

"You know better than to be up here." My father pulls me toward him. His hot breath blows on my face. "You have no business being in places you shouldn't be."

"I was just looking."

"I don't want to hear it," he says. He pulls me to the side, away from the other adults, but there is no point. They are still close enough to hear. "You disobeyed me and the council. I've already had to deal with you fighting with Marlow, but now this?"

"I had to. I had to talk to the boy again."

His eyes widen and his skin pales. "What boy?" he turns to Terrick who steps out from the other men.

Apparently, my friends didn't tell them everything.

"A boy. He was by the hills. I saw him yesterday, and today I brought him food. He was hungry and was eating rodents." I watch as they exchange glances. Their attention moves from each other to the ridgeline above the village. "We were just talking."

"About what?" Terrick asks beside my father. "What would you and a Nadeen have to talk about?"

"I told him we don't want to fight them and that I wanted to be his friend. That's all."

Terrick lowers his voice and stares at me with an intensity

that makes me want to sink into the ground. "Colfar, I need you to be very honest with me. Did you talk to him about anything else? Anything about our village? People could be in danger, Colfar. So, no matter how insignificant of a conversation you feel it was, we need to know what you said."

"I told you. I said we wanted peace and…" I know I said more but being stared at doesn't make it easier to recall my conversation.

Terrick leans forward. "And, what?"

My eyes turn downward, and I stare at his mud-covered boots. All their feet are muddy. It is evidence of the hard work they do to care for everyone here. I know my conversation concerns them, but I honestly said nothing that would harm us… I don't think.

"I said you were talking with them about getting more land."

My father tightens his grip on my elbow. "You said what?"

"I said nothing that the Nadeens wouldn't already know."

"That wasn't for you to get involved in," my father sounds out of breath. Almost as if he is panting. "Those conversations needed to be kept between myself and the Nadeens directly involved in the discussions. We don't need others influencing those negotiations."

"How could the boy—"

"I doubt he is alone up there, and if those with him disagree with giving us more land, word will get back to the city. The conversation could be over before we get to fully negotiate."

I never thought my conversation with the boy would interfere with my father's negotiations. It was only to help. "I'm sorry," I say.

"What else did you say?" Terrick asks. He crosses his arms and stares down his nose.

I take a breath, trying desperately to calm my shaking limbs. "That I wanted him to talk to you. I wanted him to see that we aren't bad people. I thought, maybe then, he would share information with us about the Nadeens. I was only trying to help you."

"By talking about things that a child shouldn't be talking about?" my father says.

"The boy thought I should talk about these things. He said they train him to fight and when he heard the children in the village only do chores, he thought we were useless. I needed to prove to him I'm not useless."

My father laughs, but not a cheerful laugh. It is a laughter brought on by disbelief. "You proved that to him by giving them information?" he says. "You were useful… to him. I can't believe you would have done such a thing, Colfar. You are smarter than this."

"I don't see how you think it wasn't smart. I was trying to get him to talk to you. I only needed him to trust me a little so he could trust you."

"That's not how these things work." My father wraps his arm around my back and pushes me back toward the village. "We're calling an emergency council meeting and you are coming with us."

One by one, the council leaders file into the meeting hall. All but Hayden scowl at me as they walk past, and I slink into the corner. I am the reason Terrick has called them here, having caused what they perceive to be more problems. I still don't understand why they are so alarmed by what I've done. Sure, there might have been Nadeens that didn't know about the negotiations, but we could still leverage my conversation with the boy. We could show the Nadeens our kindness by how we respond. This is not a bad thing.

On the walk to the meeting hall, I had tried to plead with my father to consider the benefits of my conversation. No matter what I said, he emphasized the risks I had taken. But they weren't risks. They were opportunities. If only he could see it. Now, with the rest of the leaders in the room, hopefully one of them will view it the same way as I do.

"Colfar has been going to the upper level to explore," my father says to men who shake their heads in response. "Yes, he violated the rules by being up there, and the consequences of that are something I intend to discuss with him later. For now, we need to talk about what he learned while he was up there. Colfar crossed the field and approached the hills, where he found a boy. A Nadeen."

Their faces change from scowls to expressions of worry as their eyebrows part to the side. Their faces pale and their eyes sadden. The men turn to each other and mutter words I can't make out from my darkened corner of the room. Slowly, the chatter builds in the room. A controlled panic.

"Colfar says it was a young boy," my father continues, which interrupts the frenzy. "He is about Colfar's age. The way he was talking, led Colfar to believe he could convince the boy to come back here and talk to us."

"Why was a boy all the way out here?" a man asks.

"I bet it was deliberate," another says. "I bet the child was here on a training exercise. To learn how to spy on us."

"We don't know if that's true," my father says. "Colfar said the boy was hungry and dirty. We can't rule out the possibility he left the city."

A man laughs and folds his arms. "I find it hard to believe a child could have wandered away from a well-guarded city to visit the enemy they taught him to fear. It makes more sense that the Nadeens sent him here, which is alarming if you ask me."

The room fills with the sound of multiple conversations. The men huddle together. My father speaks with Terrick, who looks in my direction. I caused this meeting to happen. I caused these conversations to take place and made people concerned… or did I?

It was the Nadeens who sent someone to our village. Had I gone up there and found nothing, they might have given me a consequence for exploring, but nothing else. This meeting… this is because of the Nadeens. If it wasn't for me, we might never have known they were sending boys, like him, to spy on us.

"It is troubling that they would send anyone here," a man says over the noise. "It doesn't matter if it was a child or an adult. The Nadeens have come too close."

Terrick clears his throat and steps away from my father. "Before we discuss this further, we must remember the Nadeens haven't attacked us. This may have been a simple attempt to gather information. They used a boy, most likely because they thought if we captured him, we wouldn't harm him."

"What if gathering information is the first step before an attack?" the first man says.

Hayden rises from his seat. "I think we shouldn't jump to

conclusions. Not yet, at least. Colfar can tell us the boy's questions and what he said. That will help us understand."

The knots in my stomach have returned. Tighter than they were before. I don't want the councilmen to question me. I have already told my father all that I can remember about the exchange, but the questioning has already begun.

"What is his name?"

"How old is he?"

"Was he alone?"

"What did he ask you?"

"What did you tell him?"

My father holds out his hand, and the questions stop. With the room now silent, I emerge from the corner and stand beside my father.

I clear my throat and try to speak as confidently as I can. "The boy didn't tell me his name. He was about my age. There was nothing he said that made me think there was anyone else. He wanted to know what I did and who you were."

Terrick stares at me. "Who we were? You didn't tell us this."

"I didn't think it was important. When I suggested he meet with you, he thought I couldn't arrange anything, so I told him my father was on the council and was talking with the Nadeens to ask for more land. I guess because I told him that, he then wanted to know if my father was in charge. I said Terrick was more in charge than anyone else. Was I wrong?"

Terrick looks at my father. I have never seen Terrick look worried before, but there was no mistaking the expression of concern on his face. Terrick turns to me and his face warms to a smile, although I feel he is masking his emotions. "Not to worry,

Colfar. I'm sure he only wanted to know who to talk to… when the time comes."

"Don't lie to the boy," calls a man from the table. His lowered, bushy eyebrows almost cover his eyes. He presses his hands against the table and rises from his chair. "They wanted information about the village and specifically asked about our leadership. All of us are in danger. Terrick is in danger. Any arguments opposing my statement will only prove to us that this leadership is naïve when the Nadeens are preparing for something."

Terrick's attention is now on the man at the table. "I am not naïve. Please consider we have a child in the room with us."

"Colfar is not an innocent child," he says. "He has met a Nadeen. He has been running around, spouting things from his mouth that he shouldn't. Colfar needs to grow up. Those around him should stop protecting him from consequences or the truth. We've done more harm than good by sheltering these kids."

My father takes a step forward and Terrick raises his hand. My father holds his position.

"Colfar is not who we are discussing here," Terrick says, calmly. "We need to keep the focus on the Nadeens. I agree with you that they are up to something. What they are doing hasn't yet become clear. It would be helpful for us if there were radio transmissions to intercept. They would give us some insight into the Nadeens' activities. Before this, we have heard nothing. There have been no radio transmissions to tip us off that they were bringing anyone near the village." He slides a stack of papers across the table. "There is nothing of concern in these transcripts. For the past few days, the conversations in the transcripts have pertained to monitoring their walls."

"Do you think the boy walked here?" my father asks. "Or was he dropped off by aircraft?"

"Colfar stated that the boy's clothes were dirty. That would point to walking."

"Or he rolled in the mud," says the man with the bushy eyebrows.

I take a step forward. "He said he was hungry," I say. The men return to scowling. They did not invite me to speak again, but I need to tell them what I know. "But… even though the boy said he was hungry, and I brought him food, he didn't eat it. He said he found something else to eat."

"Like what?" Terrick asks.

"Rodents."

"Not likely," the man says. "They have probably been feeding him and wanted to see if we were well off."

"I wanted to show him we are kind," I say. "I thought by giving him food, he would trust me and maybe agree to meet with all of you."

"You didn't think to ask us first, did you boy?" The man lowers his chin as he puffs out his chest.

My father reaches back and pushes me behind him. "Colfar's actions were well-intentioned. He had only meant to go exploring and found himself in over his head once he met up with the Nadeen boy. It would have been better had he reported finding the boy on the first day instead of trying to take matters into his own hands. What's done, is done. We need to figure out what to do with the information we have. I believe we must increase our patrols around the village. We may need to include the upper trails and keep a closer eye on the ridge."

I feel my heart rate rising. This isn't how I pictured my plan.

We should try to talk to the boy, not try to prevent him from getting comfortable with us. What if he tries to come to the village to talk to the leaders, or to find me? What will the men guarding the village do?

"Wouldn't that cause alarm among the people?" asks someone from the back of the room. "We don't want to start a panic if there isn't any need. The Nadeens could have been monitoring us for years, and this is the first time we've caught them. We should wait until we have a better understanding of what is happening."

"But what if the Nadeens do something because we caught them? They'll see our patrols." The man with the bushy eyebrows turns to face the man at the back. "Our people could be in danger. Why else would they be here? They are making plans to attack. We need to move people to the caves."

My father holds out his hands to calm the men. "We don't know if they plan to attack," he says. "We also don't know if they plan to do anything besides watch us. There is nothing stating they can't enjoy the views from their land. I have been in contact with Tarsen to begin negotiations. If he wasn't responding or if he made threats, I would share your concern. I agree that monitoring could have been going on for some time. They are still talking to us, which I must believe is a good sign."

"It still makes me very uncomfortable."

"We can understand why," Terrick says. "I don't like Nadeens being up there, no matter what their age."

"They do whatever they like," says the first man. "That is the entire problem with not having a peace agreement. Until we have one, they will continue to push us out. If we have an agreement, then we have a right to be here."

"We have a right according to who?" my father asks. "There is no higher authority to escalate to if the Nadeens revoke an agreement. We either agree or we don't. The Nadeens could disregard an agreement at any time."

"They could, but there might be folks within their own walls who would honor it. An attack might upset a few of them if they reverse it. Inner turmoil could create enough conflict that they won't be able to attack."

I return to my corner of the room and listen to them debate for another hour. The consensus is to monitor the situation and increase patrols around the village. My father will continue to negotiate with Tarsen and won't talk to the Nadeens about the boy I met in the hills, unless they bring him up first. They will keep the conversation focused on land negotiations, as to not spook the Nadeens and sabotage a potential deal.

But there is no talk about inviting the boy to come to the village. There is no mention of bringing him food or trying to befriend him. It is as if he is useless to them… just as the boy said I was. He isn't useless. Neither of us are. I still see the value in talking to him and bringing him into the village. He can still offer information. Once he is here, and they talk to him, the council will see things the same way as I do.

CHAPTER TEN

From the corner of the room, Rory, Hart, and I watch as men and women decide our fates. Terrick invited an assortment of citizens together to make a non-biased decision on how they will punish us for visiting the upper valley. For several minutes, they talk back and forth, describing our behavior around the village. Guilt pokes at my stomach as I listen to them list off my failures. I feel like I am on trial. Before this, I had thought of myself as a well-mannered child. I listen to my parents, and I do my chores. But none of that matters with many of the adults suggesting I have a reputation for getting into mischief.

"These kids need more structure." A woman dabs her forehead with a handkerchief. She has two daughters about my age. One of them is Corin, a self-centered girl who has a habit of obsessing over things… and people. Much like her mother. "They're strong boys. I don't see why they aren't being put to work instead of being allowed to run around causing trouble."

"That isn't a bad idea," Terrick says. "They are eleven-years-old now. By this age, I was already helping my father with his duties."

My father glances over his shoulder and nods. "He can hold a bucket of nails and swing a hammer. And I could use some help. It is just a shame…" He looks back at the adults around the table. "I wish they could be free to run around up there. I know I did the same thing when I was a child and they never punished me for it." He can't decide the consequence, but he can comment. Maybe he is hoping the punishment won't be too harsh.

"That is because I convinced your father and the other adults to let you off the hook," Terrick says with a wink and a laugh. "Colfar is definitely your son."

"Still," my father says, ignoring Terrick's attempt at humor, "it feels as if the times have changed. Things aren't getting better for them. It is becoming harder to be a child."

The adults nod. The mood in the room has shifted from anger to empathy. Adults stare at the ground. It is silent. I can only compare the feeling to being in a room after an attack. Like people are grieving. It isn't about our behavior anymore. It is about the war and the Nadeens.

"War or not, Aldon," Corin's mother says, breaking through the silence as she leans back in her chair, "children still need discipline. If putting them to work is what they need to keep them out of trouble, then you should keep them with you to monitor them. Put some of that pent-up energy to good use." I think she hates me.

"You're saying 'them' as if I have another child."

"Well, I only assumed you would take on Rory, since he and

Colfar are such good friends, and his father has passed on. His mother works as a seamstress, so he won't burn off much energy with a needle and thread."

Rory groans and kicks his foot against the ground. This was my fault. I got him in trouble. He shouldn't have to work because I encouraged him to explore the upper valley. They were the ones who told the adults and didn't explore with me a second time. There should be some leniency from the adults for that.

Hart lets out a loud sigh and the adults turn toward him.

"What is it, Hart?" Terrick asks. "Do you disagree with us?"

He steps forward. "It was Colfar's stupid idea. Rory and I went home without him when he wouldn't leave. He is the one that went up there twice. I don't see why we should be in trouble."

"I agree," I say, now standing beside him. "It was me who wanted to go up there and talked them into coming along. Once we were in the valley, they kept saying we shouldn't be there and wanted to go back. I asked them to keep the exploration a secret. I shouldn't have done it, and you shouldn't punish them for what I asked them to do. It is my fault."

"They made the choice to follow you," my father says. "They knew the rules and still broke them."

"But father—"

"Don't," he says, raising a finger. "We have enough to worry about. We don't need to worry about where you are. With you being up there, you could easy have undone the talks we are having with the Nadeens. How are we supposed to convince them that three boys took it upon themselves to explore the upper valley without our knowledge?"

I lower my head. "I don't know."

"Exactly. Because you weren't thinking about that, were you?" Like earlier in the day, his face is once again glowing red. His chest rises and falls. His feet shuffle. Terrick places his hand on my father's shoulder, who responds by taking longer and slower breaths. "You thought you would save the village all on your own without consulting with the adults or thinking about the consequences of your actions. I am disappointed, Colfar. Very disappointed."

I don't enjoy seeing my father this angry. He is pacing in place; he is holding back the full expression of his anger. He is choosing to limit what I see and experience, but I get the message. I don't need to see all of his anger to know I disappointed him… again.

I attempt to swallow away the lump in my throat, but it remains. The tightened muscles in my neck make my throat burn. It is a miserable feeling. I want to correct what I've done, but I don't want my efforts to become something hurtful and negative. They were to have a positive impact. "The last thing I wanted to do was make it harder for the council or put the village in any danger." My voice squeaks through my burning throat. "I wanted to help instead of sitting around doing nothing. You were talking about needing more land and when we sit up at the viewpoint, we see all this land we aren't using. It's right there. If they will attack us for being in the valley anyway, why not use the land?"

"Using that land would only anger them more," my father says. "There is no place for anyone to hide up there."

"Then just use it to grow stuff and raise animals. Move the animals away from the land we need for people and use the land the animals were on to build houses."

"And what happens when they destroy all of our food?" a man shouts. "At least having it all kept between the walls gives it some protection." He shakes his head and steps back. "I can't believe I am arguing with a child."

"We could save what we don't use in the caves," I say. I'm sure he finds it frustrating to be arguing with a child, but I am the only one making sense. "Putting excess supplies in the cave would protect it, wouldn't it?"

My father shakes his head. "You are young, Colfar. I don't expect you to understand all the complexities involved."

"I'm trying to understand. That's why I went up there. You've told me about the land, but I haven't seen it for myself."

He steps closer. "What you're saying is you didn't trust us. We said not to go up there. That was all you needed to know."

How does he not understand? My age shouldn't matter. I can't blindly listen to what I'm told. I need to make my own decisions about things with facts and not opinions. "Maybe it is time to give the kids more information, besides telling us what not to do. I don't want anyone to treat me like a child anymore."

My father inhales, and I watch his face. I am not falling in line and it makes him angry. I'm also arguing with him in front of a room full of adults. But I will no longer take people's word as truth when I need to understand the reasoning for something.

"I don't appreciate you talking back." My father's voice rings in my ears. The adults turn away, averting their eyes from our conversation. "I have told you what you need to know. It is not safe. The Nadeens don't want us up there—"

"They don't want us down here either. What's the difference?"

"The difference is… this is our home. This is what we

protect. We decided we won't do anything that would anger the Nadeens. They have stated that if we set foot up there, they will bring a consequence down on us. You went up there. I am holding my breath now, waiting for them to take action."

"You think they will attack us because I went up there?"

"An attack is a real possibility."

Corin's mother clears her throat. "As I mentioned before, these boys lack discipline. Just look at the way he is speaking to his father. A little extra work may make a significant difference."

The adults nod and chatter to each other. Terrick pulls on my father's shoulder. He leans back as Terrick whispers in his ear. Corin's mother stares at me, stern-faced, while Rory and Hart stand to the side, avoiding eye contact with anyone in the room.

My father tugs on the bottom of his shirt and turns to the adults. "I agree with you," he says. "If you agree, I will take Rory and Colfar with me to work on construction efforts today and they can continue into the future. Hart can work in the blacksmith shop with his father. If they are being truthful when they say they want to help the village, then this can be their contribution. There will be no need to worry themselves about other business that is taking place, especially if they use their time for work."

I kick at the ground. I used my time for work. What I was doing was important. Making me work on construction doesn't make the Nadeen boy go away. It doesn't take away his hunger. I am to bring him food tomorrow. The only comfort I have is to know the work won't last all day. Once the work is over, I will continue what I have started. It will tire me, but I will do the work the adults want me to do and I will continue to help the boy. I promised him more food, and I will keep my word.

"Even though it isn't under the best of circumstances," my father says, "I am happy to have you boys working with me today. With the extra hands, we will build these homes faster." Standing by a stack of pre-cut wooden boards, he places his hands on his hips and leans to the side to stretch his back. "In the next couple of days, the two of you will become good builders."

"But we don't know what we're doing," I say, as I pick up the hammer and feel its weight in my hands.

My father lifts a board from an arranged stack and carries it toward the worksite. "You'll learn quick enough," he says. "Grab a board and follow me."

I drop the extra hammer and Rory and I each slide a board from the stack, then follow my father. The long board teeters in my hands. Its end drags in the dirt behind me. Rory also struggles. Having tucked the board under his arm, the front-end slams into the ground and digs into the dirt, bringing him to a halt.

"These are heavy," Rory says, lifting it from the ground.

My father looks over his shoulder and smiles. "That, they are. Soon you will build up enough muscle to carry multiple boards at once."

In the distance, I see a man with a stack of boards balanced on his shoulder. It will still be a few years before I can balance wood on my shoulder like him. At my size, my body could collapse under the weight. For now, the board drags along the ground while its roughly cut edges dig into the palm of my hands.

I copy my father and drop the board in front of a newly

constructed wooden frame. This will become someone's new home. The wood smells fresh. As there are no extra materials to repurpose, they have cut trees to create the needed supplies.

Men are hard at work driving nails into the beams. It is a small house. With only one bedroom, they are not building it for a large family. I think about the names of those who are waiting for a solid home and try to think of who they intend this house for. At least seven small families come to mind.

"Colfar," my father calls from the open doorway. "I need you and Rory to bring ten more boards each. Pile them at the door with the others. I'll tell you what else to do when you're done."

"Ten?" Rory asks, with a waver to his voice.

"Ten," my father repeats.

I sigh and walk back to the stack of wood to drag off another board. Moving wood from one location to another is not what I pictured myself doing. If they are making me work at the construction site, I could at least do something that will help people, such as using a hammer. I want to build, not gather supplies.

Again, the board drags behind me, carving a trench in the dirt. I lift it from the ground and feel the weight shift, pushing me forward. I lean back to balance and the board is back to striking the ground.

"Pick up your board, Colfar," Rory says with a cough. "You're putting dust in the air."

"Sorry." His complaint has come a little late. I'm already at the door and I toss the board on top of the pile. Rory catches up and slides his in place. "I hope we don't have to carry wood every day," I say.

Rory is the first to pick up his next board. "It will be boring if this is all your father will have us do." Soon his board is on the pile, but we still have eight more to go.

"My mother said she will bring us lunch this afternoon. I think this is the first time in ages I don't have to bring lunch to my father."

Rory claps his hands together to remove the dust. There is no point in dusting them off when we still need to gather eight boards. "It must feel strange to have your mother bring you lunch. It is as if you're really working."

"I am really working. And it sounds like this is how every day will be for a long while."

Rory groans and I try not to copy him. It is frustrating to have work be given to us as a consequence. I wanted to help, but I wanted to volunteer to do it. I never pictured being forced to because we upset the adults. In my imagination, they were pleased I stepped up and wanted to contribute. I don't, however, want the adults to think I have a negative attitude about it. This work could lead to other opportunities. Something better than this.

Before I know it, we have moved each of our ten boards and my father steps out of the doorway to inspect our work.

"Well done," he says. "Come inside." We follow him through the door, which seems ridiculous as much of the front has no walls. Someone has laid only a few floorboards across the beams and dirt remains visible below. "Grab those nails." He points to a metal bucket perched on the floor's frame in the corner.

I balance on the wooden beams to grab the bucket and balance, once again, to return to Rory and my father.

"Hold this board steady," he says to Rory as they hold a flat floorboard against an already secured plank. "Don't move." My father takes a nail from the bucket and strikes it with a hammer through the wood. "Colfar, your turn. Put a nail in beside that one."

"Here?" I ask, positioning my nail close to the other.

My father takes my hand and slides it a toward the opposite side of the board. "Spread them apart a bit. Go ahead."

I swing my hammer. Afraid I will strike my hand, I slow my arm before striking the nail. I strike the nail which stands straight in the board. It is not deep in the wood. It only sunk in part of the way.

"Hit it again until it is through."

I do as I'm told, striking the nail until it is in place.

"Good," he says. "The two of you can take turns hammering in these boards. When you reach the point when you need to cut a board to make it fit, come and find me."

I look at Rory, who has already moved to the far end of the board with a hammer lifted in the air. I put my weight against the board, and he swings.

Finally, I can build. Taking turns, we make quick work of the floorboards, laying a flat floor in the home. We sit with our backs against the wall, admiring our work and smile. Someone will live in this home soon and they will walk on this floor. The floor I helped Rory to install. They will place their furniture around the room and children will play here. They will fill it with happiness because they have a place to live. We will have helped to give them that place. This work is something to be proud of.

It doesn't matter how I found myself here. I can see myself doing this when I am older. It could be fun and rewarding. Hopefully, Rory has also enjoyed putting this floor together as I wouldn't mind continuing to work with him. Over time, we can learn from my father how to build the framing and the roofing. For today, I feel pride in having learned how to put the floor in place, but there is so much more to learn.

"Well done, boys," my father says, stepping on the freshly laid floor. "It seems you have a gift for construction. This is splendid work. Ava," he calls over his shoulder. "Come look at this."

My mother steps through the door with our lunches in her hands. "Oh. How lovely. The Macnolls will be so happy with this when they see it."

The Macnolls. They are the family who will one day occupy by the house. The ones who will walk on this floor. The first family I have helped in the village.

CHAPTER ELEVEN

With the required work out of the way, I am left with the rest of my afternoon to focus on the Nadeen boy at the hills. Hopefully, my delay will have no impact on the progress I've made. All day, I have imagined him sitting on the boulder wondering if I have been ignoring him. After our last encounter and suggesting he meet with the leaders, I have left him alone to question my intentions.

I have told no one my plans. Not even Rory or Hart know that I will visit the boy today. Since the council spoke to me, I have spent the day doing chores and they should all think I will stay away from here. There is no reason to think I would go up here again. They won't know that I have, unless I return with the boy. If he doesn't come, it will remain my secret.

With one last check over my shoulder, I determine that no one has seen me, and I make my way up the hill. I watch the men patrolling in the distance, monitoring their patterns on the opposite site of the village. They will check for movement on the slope. If they see me climbing the hill, they will notify my father and the other council members. They won't know who I am until they get close. Who knows what chaos I could cause? They could draw weapons. Others could ring the alarms. There is no saying what my consequence would be if they catch me a second time.

At the top of the slope, I crouch to get a last glimpse of the men patrolling the outer edges of the village. No one has moved from their patrol boundaries. I exhale. They must be unaware I am here. I hunch over and rush through the field. I need to make this a quick visit. If I am gone too long, someone will eventually notice I am missing. I have only a short amount of time to convince the boy to return with me.

To my relief, the boy is on the boulder, lying on the rock and looking up at the sky. I am still a way off when he rolls onto his stomach to face me.

"You're still here," I shout with a wave.

"Where else would I be?" he asks, now sitting up.

Finding a nearby rock, I sit down with a view of the boy above me. "I wondered if you would have gone home. I thought if I didn't come back, you'd maybe give up on me."

He pivots and dangles both legs over the edge of the boulder. "I waited."

"I'm glad you did. The adults had me working on building houses, so I didn't get to bring you any food today."

"You promised food. Why did you come back then?" he asks.

"I wanted to talk to you about coming to the village and maybe talking to the leadership."

"I am not interested in that." He looks toward the village and back at me. His eyes narrow and then relax.

I don't know how I will convince him to come with me. I

have nothing to offer him as an incentive. He has no interest in coming to the village and the adults don't want to meet with him. Maybe there is no point in me being here, not if there is no hope he would follow me home.

The boy tilts his head and gives a slow nod. "Where are the adults now?" he asks.

"They're all working."

He shakes his head. "I mean the leaders. Your father and the other man you mentioned… Terris?"

"Terrick," I say smiling.

"Yes, that was his name. Where is Terrick now? Are they meeting?"

I look toward the village. My father hadn't really said if they were meeting again. It would make sense that they would, if he could talk to that Nadeen, Tarsen, again.

"Yes or no?" the boy shouts at me. He tilts his head to the side again and holds his hand to his ear.

He touched his head yesterday when I spoke with him. I take a step forward. "What are you doing?" I ask.

He stares at me. "None of your business."

I lean to the side and stand on my toes, straining to get a better look. He turns away.

"I want to know why you keep touching your ear."

"So, what?" he asks, lowering his hand to his side. "Do you want me to come down to the village to meet with your leaders, or not?"

My emotions swing from the soaring feeling of excitement to the sickening feeling of fear. He will come to the village, but there is something in his ear. Is someone talking to him?

He presses his hand to the side of this head. "Am I to meet with them now, or not?"

My mind is full of thoughts. Who is he? Does he really want to meet with them? He keeps asking. He needs an answer.

"You can," I say.

"Are the leaders meeting now?" he asks.

"I believe so," I reply.

He raises his hand and holds it against his ear. "Go now," he says. He stares at me with narrowed eyes and a frightening smirk.

"Go where?"

He smiles. "I was talking to them." He points behind me, toward the sky. Two dark aircraft screech overhead. Moving fast, they are on a direct path to the village.

I feel the blood drain from my face. I want to scream and warn the council, or anyone who can hear my cries. Most of all, I want to beat the boy who lied. But, there is no time. Without another thought, I turn toward the village and run.

From the upper valley, I watch the aircraft cross over the village and open fire. Plumes of dirt lift into the air above the horizon. In a few more feet, I will look down into the valley and see which buildings they struck. A small pillar of smoke climbs toward the sky. It thickens and darkens with each puff.

At the edge of the slope, I freeze. A black cloud of smoke rises from the northern side of the village. The Nadeens have struck the meeting hall and the buildings beside it.

Air escapes my lungs and my vision blurs. I grab my legs to steady myself. My father and the other councilors could have been inside. From this distance, I can't see any activity around the structure. All I see are people running in all directions along the streets as a larger aircraft approaches in the distance. Several other smaller aircraft fly beside it. It is a large, black mothership with short wings sticking out from its sides. Soon, there will be even more destruction.

As the mothership draws closer, the aircraft's size is even more apparent. A low rumble fills the valley, and a wind kicks up around me. I rush down the slope, sliding down the dirt, slowing only when snagged by protruding rocks.

Between the walls of the valley, it is chaos. People run toward the caves. The screams of adults and children make my ears ring. Smoke has filled the air. My village is under attack.

Cupping my hands over my ears, I run into the crowd, searching for the faces of my parents. If my father isn't still inside the flattened meeting hall, he will be busy helping people get to safety. My mother will do the same, while keeping watch for me.

"Father?" I shout into the crowd. "Mother?"

The crowd continues to run down the road. My parents are not among them. I weave between a row of homes, to the next road where more people run toward the caves. I know what my parents would want me to do. They would want me to follow the sea of fleeing adults and hide in the caves. I can't. Not until I find them.

An explosion to my left sends me to the ground. The many small aircraft that once flanked the mothership have broken away and swoop down at the village, firing randomly. The next wave of the attack has begun. We are now moving targets with automatic fire tearing up the dirt around those attempting to reach safety. I scramble to my feet and run toward the bridge connecting the southern half of the village to the caves on the other side.

The Nadeens continue to pound at the village, striking at

buildings. The explosions send clouds of smoke and dirt into the air.

I cover my face with no effect. Particles enter my lungs and choke me. I cough. A distant explosion erupts to my right. The crowd veers left and a large man crashes into me. We tumble to the ground, knocking over several small, wooden crates on the way down. My knee catches the corner of a box. It has left a large gash in my pants and has cut through my skin. I pull my leg toward me to examine the wound. It stings as blood pools and dribbles down my leg calf.

I sniffle and take a quick breath. When my mother finishes helping the dying and other wounded, she will bandage my cut for me. I will be fine. Compared to what others will experience, my injury is nothing. I will be lucky to only have a gash on my leg. Who knows how many are already dead?

Another wave begins. Aircraft swoop down, firing into the crowd. People scatter, dodging bullets, and taking cover under what objects they can find. Someone lands behind me and pushes me against the crates.

"Keep your head down," he shouts.

I was already low to the ground. His audible instruction was for his own benefit. I've already lived through several attacks. I know what I'm doing. One needs to keep their head covered and remain out of sight until they can see the back of the aircraft.

A shop explodes to our right, and debris rains down on us. The man runs, and I am alone behind the crates once again. If he had cared, he would have encouraged me to run with him. Only his life matters now.

An aircraft screeches by, chasing after the crowd on the road. I look over my shoulder and spot my father handing off a wounded woman to a passerby. He shouts orders to a man before he disappears through a cloud of smoke.

"Father," I shout as I rise from my hiding place. Another aircraft flies by, drowning out my cries, and I duck until it passes.

When the sky is clear, I run up the road. Now I have seen my father and I know he is okay, but I need to see him again. Maybe I can help him.

I fight my way up the stream of wide-eyed people until I reach the burned-out shell of the shop where I had last seen my father. There is no sign of him. He has moved on, most likely to find others in need.

"Out of my way, child." A woman pushes past me. My heel catches a rock and I stumble backward to the ground.

"Don't just sit there in everyone's way," another man shouts as he pulls me to my feet, only to shove me to the side and out of his way. These people don't care about me. They care about themselves. There are only a few people who would stop to help rather than run, and they are out here… somewhere. Those are the people I want to be like. Today, I will follow their example. I am not heading to the caves to protect myself. Not yet. Not until I have to.

The wind from the mothership blows choking smoke toward me, and I cover my watering eyes. I hurry down the battered roads. The blasts have exposed the roots from trees cleared from the valley years ago. People step through the craters, clawing their way back onto level ground. Families help loved ones through the piles of dirt and debris, trying desperately to reach the caves at the other end of the village.

I move against the flow of the crowd. People turn their heads as I pass by, most likely confused by my direction.

I turn to the right, toward other intact buildings. They are now the focus of the Nadeens' new wave of attacks. People limp past, helped by others who support them.

"Colfar, get to the caves," I hear to my left. My father has freed a man from a pile of burning debris and guides him toward the road. "Get going," he shouts at me before a burning beam gives way. The roof crashes to the ground, spraying sparks and embers into the surrounding air. My father lifts his arms to cover his face and I watch the sparks strike his skin.

I run forward, desperately wanting to pull him away. The roof could have hit him.

"Go!" he shouts, stepping back from the building. "Get to safety. I'm fine."

I stop and take one last look at my father, who has returned to focus on the blaze and his search for victims. My being here is a distraction. He has work to do and his calls shift his focus from the dangers. I look over my shoulder toward the caves and do as I am told.

I run.

Only a few feet later, I am stopped by the sound of a choking cough. To my left is a girl, surrounded by smoke as she holds her hands to her face. She looks at me. Her eyes are red and irritated. I know her. It was her mother who pushed my father to give Rory, Hart, and I consequences for visiting the upper valley. Now, her daughter needs me.

"Corin?" I call out. "Come on, Corin. Take my hand." Her watering eyes are wide. She shakes her head and holds her hand to her chest. As she looks up and down the street at the burning shops, it is clear she is disoriented and doesn't know which way to go. "Corin. I know where the caves are. I can help you." I step into the smoke and grab her hand. She doesn't resist me and I pull her down the road.

An aircraft flies over us, and I hold her against the side of the building. She trembles beside me.

"He didn't see us," I say. "It's okay." I see no reaction.

I give her hand a squeeze and pull her back onto the road. Soon, we are over the bridge, to the mouth of the cave. Men stand at the entrance and usher everyone inside. I release Corin's hand and push her forward. She turns to look back at me.

"Go on, Corin," I say.

A man reaches out to guide me into the cave, and I pivot away, avoiding his grasp.

"Get inside," he shouts. "You need to take cover."

"Not yet," I say, and I run back toward the bridge, crossing over the chasm to the village.

After helping Corin, I know what I need to do. There will be others who need me. Even my father. I haven't seen my mother yet, although I must assume she is already in the caves tending to the wounded.

Another aircraft returns and I cover my head, crouching low to the ground. More buildings explode ahead of me and people scream. The smoke thickens and people step through the dark cloud, searching for fresh air.

"The caves are that way," I shout, pointing behind me. Even if all I do is direct people to the caves, that's enough. I'm doing something.

They nod and run past. Some carry injured people in their arms while others cover their faces, masking their shock.

Screeches and explosions repeat, drowning out the cries of the injured. The Nadeens focus their aircraft on the same section of the village, relentlessly opening fire. Why? Have they spotted something of interest? People? The rescuers? My father?

I run toward the smoke and an aircraft breaks away from its pack. Flying toward me, it fires at the bridge, striking the ground nearby. The blast digs up the dirt around the support posts and I gasp. Flames have erupted on the wood and ropes.

"No," I whisper under my breath. Without the bridge, the Nadeens will cut people off from the caves and from safety.

People, once running for the caves, now scatter. They have abandoned their attempt to reach the bridge and now hide behind whatever sources of protection they can find. Crates, rain barrels, woodpiles. Whatever they feel might make themselves invisible to the Nadeens, they position themselves behind.

"We have to save the bridge," I shout. "We have to get people to the other side." I run to a nearby shop's rain barrel and find a bucket to toss into the water. "Get a bucket," I yell to the frightened people. Running back to the bridge, I empty the bucket onto the blaze and rush back to the barrel for more. "Move. Before it burns down."

They have misunderstood me. They cross the bridge. I watch the weakened posts lean under the weight of the crowd. I need more workers, but none of them stop to help me douse the flames. If we allow the ropes to continue to burn, they will snap. Who knows when we will have time to repair it? Even worse, it will trap the wounded on the southern-most side, without medical supplies. Many will die.

I run back to the barrel, filling another bucketful of water. With a swing of my arms, water flies from my bucket, wetting the bridge, but it barely touches the rising flames. Again, I run back to the barrel, but something blocks my bucket. Another bucket is being filled… by Marlow. He pulls his full bucket from the barrel and I sink mine into the water before we run together toward the bridge.

"Just this once, I will help you," Marlow says, tossing his bucket of water at the flames. "I will not let people die because I don't like you."

"Thank you," I say. My bucket is empty again. Marlow has already returned to the rain barrel. I run back for more water.

We make several trips, working together in our battle against the flames. Aircraft continue to fly over the village. My hands shake as I grip the bucket. My father is out there. After the conversation with the boy at the hills, I know now that my father is a target. Why else would the boy have asked such questions about the leaders? I have no time to dwell on it. A blast to our left forces Marlow and I to the ground, spilling our buckets and soaking the ground.

An aircraft zooms toward us. I suspect the Nadeens have spotted our efforts.

"Run," I shout. We scramble to our feet and run toward a smoking pile of rubble. The aircraft circles back and fires at the bridge.

"No!" I shout.

The aircraft misses, striking the ground on both sides of the ravine before it flies back to the others.

I grab at Marlow's elbow. "Come on," I say. "We need to get those flames out."

Marlow runs behind me and we grab our buckets. We fill them quickly and return to the bridge, tossing more water onto the remaining flames. Having already dampened the bridge, our previous efforts have slowed the burn, although we have not yet extinguished the flames.

"We've almost got it," Marlow cheers.

The aircraft screeches up behind us, and we lie on our bellies, waiting for the strike. It doesn't fire on us, or the bridge. It swoops upward, toward the approaching mothership. Marlow and I look up and watch as the underside of the mothership parts and the aircraft slows, slipping up into the belly of the ship and out of view. From all directions, other aircraft fly toward the mothership. One by one, they all return into the belly. The underside creaks and the doors close with a finishing rattle. The wind whips up around us. Dirt blows into my mouth and eyes. I gag and place my arm over my face.

The mothership roars and drifts over the village. They must be inspecting the damage they have inflicted on us.

The attack is over.

I rise to my feet and grab my bucket. There are still a few smaller flames needing to be extinguished, and I will not let the Nadeens watch our bridge fall. With Marlow beside me, we toss buckets of water at the bridge until the fire is out. We continue pouring water for some time, searching for hot spots on the boards. Finally, I drop my bucket and sink to the ground and watch the mothership disappear into the distance. I wonder if the boy is inside. If so, could he see me? Was this the plan all along?

I hear screams as people who had been hiding, now run through the streets toward the bridge.

"Get out of their way, Marlow," I shout.

He steps off the bridge with his bucket to allow the stampede across. They watch the skies, turning back to note the position of the mothership. I search their faces. Still, none of them are my family.

"Has anyone seen my father?" I shout.

They don't answer. He still isn't here. If he has found injured people, he will help them to safety.

"Do you want me to help you look for him?" Marlow asks.

I shake my head.

"My mother?" I shout to the crowd. "Have you seen her?" Still no response.

"I saw her," Marlow says. "She was with Ralda at the start of the attack, carrying some packages toward the caves." She and Ralda have always worked together to help the wounded. It would make sense that Marlow would have seen her.

"Come on," Marlow says as we cross the bridge into the safety of the caves. "Let's go find your mother."

CHAPTER TWELVE

Men at the entrance usher Marlow and me through the mouth of the cave. The crush and flow of people pushes us deeper through the corridor, into the main cavern. Dust kicked up by people and the earlier explosions still lingers in the air, in search of a place to settle. Even though we are safe behind the walls, adults and children continue to cry. They cling to boulders and to each other. Small rocks, loosened by the blasts, periodically fall from the ceiling. People look up, expecting the ceiling to collapse and bury us all alive. After the many years of attacks, it hasn't caved in yet. It has been solid and stable.

I have hidden here many times before, and each time the experience has been just as frightening. My heart races as I join the new arrivals in a search for an empty corner to wait in. Quickly, I realize people have already occupied all the spaces near the front of the cave. There will be more space deeper inside on the various levels that surround the central open cavity, a pit that extends high above our heads and deep below the main entrance.

To the left of the corridor is a large enclave. This is where the leaders and rescuers, including my father, will gather and rest. By positioning themselves there, people know where to find them and they can gather for meetings.

"I need to find Barret," Marlow says. He darts to the right and disappears down a winding path in search of his younger brother.

In a cave full of people, I am alone in my search for my family and a place to remain out of the way. Peering into the enclave, it is empty. The rescuers are outside, too busy to rest. Sleeping cots are in place, reserved and ready for their arrival. The men will keep working until there is no one left to assist, or until they are ready to collapse from exhaustion.

The caves groan as dirt and rocks continue to settle. The screams return. I crouch down, covering my head, protecting myself from the expected shower of dirt and rock, but none comes.

"We're all going to die in here," a man shouts.

"No, we're not." It is my father, helping to ease a man with an injured leg to the floor. A mixture of dirt and soot has covered their clothing and skin. The man grabs at his leg as medics gather around him.

My father places his hands on his hips and stretches his back. "We're all going to be fine as long as we stick together, and we follow instructions. In here, you are safe. The walls of the cave are strong. We have plenty of supplies inside ready to use. Protect your heads from loose rocks and remain calm, especially for the children."

I push my way toward him. I want to hug him and check he is okay. I wave to him, but the flow of people blocks me from his view. I reach my hand out to his. He doesn't notice and turns before slipping away into the crowd.

"Colfar," calls a voice from behind. It is Terrick. "Find Ralda and your mother. I'm sure they could use some help. Get them whatever supplies they ask for."

I glance back toward the entrance. My father has left to find more injured people. My legs shake and my stomach churns. The Nadeens could still return, and he would be an open target.

Terrick's hand is on my shoulder. "Colfar. Are you alright?"

I look up at him. "Will he rest soon?"

Terrick smiles and bends down. "Your father will rest soon enough. There are still many who need help to reach the cave. Go help your mother with the people your father has brought in. I need to help him."

Terrick gives me a light push forward and I follow the path away from the enclave. I will return later to, hopefully, find my father. It is hard not to think about my father running through smoke and fire after he barely avoided the Nadeens who were trying to kill him. Noting the number of people in the caves, I know there are still many more the rescuers have yet to find.

Further into the caves, the wounded line the walls. Moving closer, their injuries become clearer and the details more gruesome. Among the skilled volunteers and medics attending to the injured are Ralda and my mother, rushing from the unconscious to the wailing and bleeding victims. Blood has soaked my mother's clothes. Her hair is a mess, having fallen out of the clasp she had used to secure it behind her head. Victims take up floor space around her and she watches the ground as she navigates between broken and bloodied limbs.

"Mom," I shout over the screams.

My mother turns and moves through the bodies to reach my side. She grabs my shoulders. "Oh, Colfar. You're okay. I heard people had seen you come inside."

"Terrick said I should come help you. Bring you supplies if you need them."

She looks over her shoulder to Ralda, who is busy bandaging a head wound. "That would be wonderful. Go to the crates by the wall and grab us more bandages. Then, see if you can find us a couple buckets of water."

"Ava," Ralda shouts as she descends on a woman coughing up blood near the wall. "I need you."

My mother rushes away, and I run toward the crates. Bandages. My mother needs bandages.

The once steady flow of people entering the caves has slowed. Those arriving have greater injuries and rescuers carry them in their arms or on stretchers. I fear some won't survive. The volunteers struggle to keep up with the casualties. The faces of once optimistic medics have transformed into despair as they recognize the futility of their efforts. The wounds are too severe. The supplies and their skills too limited to treat them. The medics are losing the battle and people are dying.

Medics run from person to person, slowing their bleeding and providing them comfort. It is easy for me to spot when someone has died. The medics don't help the dead. Instead, they step around them and avert their eyes. No one wants to look at the bodies. It is too difficult to see the vacant faces of people you once knew.

On the ground, I see the bodies of children I once played with now lying beside their lifeless parents. They most likely died together, trying to protect each other.

I used to cry when I saw the dead. Not anymore. There is no time to dwell on sadness when you are trying to be helpful. If I cry, they will send me to sit with the other children. Adults desperate to distract the little ones in the cave will supervise me. I am too old and aware of the dangers. They can't distract me. And so, I need to not cry.

The medics and volunteers don't stop working. For hours, they have cared for people and not once have I seen them stop to eat or rest. The only change is the speed in which they move. They are slower now. Either they feel the remaining injured have stabilized enough, or the caregivers are now too tired to respond as quickly as they had.

Regardless of the reason, I know what I can do to help. I can bring them food. They may refuse what I bring, but I will make sure that the medics and volunteers have something available to eat. It is what Ralda would do if she wasn't still busy applying bandages.

I follow the stone path along the central cavity, down into the lower levels of the cave. Among crates of vegetables and breads, I find a team hard at work preparing food for distribution.

"May I take a few of these to the medics?" I ask, standing

beside a basket of bread. "They are looking tired and hungry. I thought a little food might help."

"You are Aldon and Ava's son, aren't you?" a woman asks.

I shift my gaze to the ground. Given the reputation have I made for myself lately, being known as their son might not be a good thing. "I am," I say. "They are busy helping and I want to do something, too."

She nods and points to a basket. "Take what you need. If they need more, come back and get some."

"Thank you. If you need me to help hand this out to others, I can do that."

"Only if your mother and father don't need you. We would appreciate the help. There are many hungry people around here."

I nod and take an armful of food before scurrying back up the rocky path.

The medics have fewer people to tend to now. That may not be a good thing.

I spot my mother leaning against a wall. Her eyes are closed as she steals a moment to rest. In the past, I've seen the volunteers work in a rotation as there are less needing care. But my mother says this is the most difficult time for the volunteers. When things are quiet, they reflect on the lives they couldn't save. She says she would rather be busy and not sleep than think about those they'd lost.

Kneeling beside my mother, I nudge her shoulder and hold out a bread roll.

"Oh, Colfar. Thank you." With her blood-stained hands, she tears off a piece of bread from the roll and points me toward Ralda.

I offer food to each medic and volunteer until all have either taken their share or refused. What I have left, I give to families who sit with their injured or dead loved ones. My gesture feels insignificant considering what they've been through.

Once my arms are empty, I head back down the path to grab a distribution basket and deliver food to the other waiting families in the caves. Many refuse, having lost their family members and their appetites during the attack.

I come across a young boy hiding under his mother's arm. He buries his face into her side. I hold out a piece of bread.

"Here you go."

He pushes his face against his mother and pulls her shirt over his ear.

"Aren't you hungry?"

His mother reaches out her hand and takes the bread. "He lost many friends today," she says. "He doesn't feel like eating, but he may soon. Thank you."

I know what it feels to lose friends. I have lost many over the years. And then my thoughts turn to Rory and Hart. I haven't seen them since before the attack. I last saw Rory when we were helping with the construction. Bile rises to my throat.

As I run down the path, people hold out their hands, hoping I will stop to hand out the food in the basket. I can see the disappointment on their faces as I continue past them. I can't stop when I don't know if my friends have made it to the caves alive. The corner to the right is where they have taken cover in the past. I stop. A family huddles in their corner. There are no signs of Rory or Hart.

I drop the basket and a family scrambles to collect the remaining food. I don't even care if they get more than their share.

I continue further up the path. If Rory or Hart have come this way and found a family occupied their spot, the current of people would have pushed them further into the cave until they found a vacancy. At every corner, I stop and check the faces. The deeper I search, the more disheartened I become. My mouth dries and my limbs increase in weight. I reach a dead end and turn around to head back toward the medics.

My throat tightens. I don't want to search the bodies or the injured. I need to remember that I haven't, yet, looked for them in the lower levels of the cave. If I don't find them there or with the medics, I will fear the rubble has trapped them outside and they are waiting for someone to rescue them.

Victims cram the space in the cave. Inconsiderate people stand in my way and others stretch their legs into the path. Once the initial wave of arrivals is over, most people don't move around inside and will no longer be in my way, but I don't have time to wait. I need to find my friends now or alert the rescuers.

At the bottom of the path, the council has gathered outside of the enclave. Among them is my father. A darker layer of dirt and soot coats his skin.

"Father," I call out. "Have you seen Rory or Hart?"

He takes a step away from the council members. "No. They could be helping to sort supplies. I know they were asking for some able-bodied young men to open crates and move them around."

"Where is that?"

"Down three levels."

If they aren't there…

They need to be there. I don't want to think about what I'll do if I don't find them. My father would never let me go outside of the caves to search. He would send out the rescuers and my father would join them. I would stand inside the cave looking out at my burning village, hoping they find my friends alive and that none of the rescuers return injured.

Just as my father said, on the third level, a team is busy unpacking crates full of blankets and clean clothing. People line up with their arms outstretched, waiting to receive goods to bring back to their families. I don't see Rory or Hart among them. In the back, groups unstack the crates, organizing the supplies into piles. Finally, among them, I spot Rory. With a metal bar, he pries open a wooden lid from the crate and looks inside.

"Rory." I run toward him. He lets the lid fall.

"Colfar."

I wrap my arms around my friend. "I was worried. I couldn't find you on the upper levels."

"Someone was in my spot."

"I saw. My father suggested I look down here. I was afraid you were still outside."

"Nope," he says smiling. "I've been down here helping the entire time. Sorry to make you worry. Hart is with his mother, if you were wondering."

A man grabs us both by the shoulders. "If you boys could finish up your talking, we have some blankets and mats for the council. We need to get some of them sleeping sooner than later."

I remember the last time there was an attack. My father and several others worked until it was late, then took turns sleeping so they had the energy to help others.

"Right away," I say. I am happy to help them get the rest they deserve.

Rory and I scoop up a set of bedding supplies and walk back up the path to find the council inside the enclave. Three men lie on the already prepped mats, trying to rest before their next shift. My father stands with Terrick, drawing a map in the dirt, marking the places they have yet to search for victims.

Not wanting to disturb an important conversation, I tip-toe past them and pass a set of blankets to a man sitting on the ground. Immediately, he gets to work preparing his bed, quickly covering himself. I glance back at my father. He sees me and nods. It feels good to have his approval. I am giving people what they need, instead of sitting in a corner of the cave trying not to get in the way. Even if I can't be out there searching, I can at least help those who are. In my way, I am contributing to the rescue efforts.

Rory and I return to gather more blankets and mats for distribution, moving on to the oldest of our population. The seniors with their weak bodies can't sleep on the cold, rock-covered ground. Some need help onto their mats and we cover them with wool blankets. They take my hand, giving it a firm shake to express their gratitude.

We give top priority to the injured. If they are to heal well, their bodies need rest, which they won't find on the ground. As I can't move any of the wounded on my own, I leave a pile of blankets and mats outside of the care area for the medics and volunteers to distribute as they see fit.

Here, my mother continues her watch over the sickest of the injured. I wish she would rest. The few moments she could have to herself were not enough. Even in the dark, I can see she is pale. The shadows accentuate the dark circles under her eyes. The desperation I see on her face tells me she values the lives of the people here more than her own need for rest. She will sleep when they are stable, but not before. I only hope she doesn't become one of the sick because she has worked too hard.

"Colfar," Ralda shouts from the end of the room. She hands me a bundle of cloth from the floor. "Take these bandages to your father. I suspect some men may have cut themselves digging through the rubble. I'd like them to clean their wounds and cover them with these."

"I will."

Rescuing others is dangerous work. Searching the burning rubble for survivors puts them at risk of injury. The burning structures are not stable, and buildings have collapsed on rescuers before. Pieces of debris are jagged, and injuries are common. They need to be cautious and take care of themselves.

I find my way to my father, alone on a mat in the far corner of the enclave. I step around the sleeping rescuers and lower myself beside him.

"Ralda asked me to bring you this."

"Thank you," he says, reaching for the bundle. A mix of soot, mud, and blood covers his hands. His blood oozes from several minor cuts.

"You're hurt," I say.

He smiles. "These will heal. She should have saved these bandages for the others."

"But you're injured, too."

He shakes his head and holds out his hands. "There are people who are far more injured than I am. You've seen them yourself."

I nod and stare at my father's blood-covered hands. I know some blood isn't his, but I hate to know something has hurt him. I wrap my arms around him, and he slips his arm over my shoulders. For the first time since the attack, I feel safe.

CHAPTER THIRTEEN

As the sun crests the horizon, its light illuminates the smoke that continues to rise from the shells of burned-out homes. It billows and soars like columns up into the sky. Rory and I sit at the viewpoint watching weary rescuers as they move from rubble pile to rubble pile, in search of survivors… and the dead. I'm sure there is no one left to rescue. I can't imagine what it would be like to survive under the debris, hurting, and waiting for rescuers. All they will find is bodies tangled in the rubble.

There is nothing for the children to do today besides stay in the corners of the cave and remain out of the way. We can't bandage wounds, so they rule us out for helping the injured. The adults have deemed the rubble unsafe for us to help clear away. We have already distributed supplies while others have already prepared meals. Everyone has their roles to get things done. All we can do is watch, wait, and wish we can be a part of the rescue effort.

I stare down at the damage. My community is hurting, and I feel miserable over being told I am too young to do anything about it. I have two hands that could help with physical labor. I helped my father construct the house and delivered food and supplies in the caves. There are tasks they could give me. Instead, I am kept from doing anything. It appears the Nadeen boy was right. I am useless.

As I choke back a sob, I hear a wail echo off the valley walls. The wailing grows, and I am reminded there are others suffering a greater loss than being able to contribute alongside the adults.

The air carries the cries through the mouth of the caves and into the village. I hate the caves and the sounds within. Even with lights strung from the ceiling, it is dim and frightening with cries multiplying and echoing, creating a roar. The smells are even worse. The number of people huddled inside increase the cave's temperature to increase, while the stench of warm vomit fills the air.

I am happy to be outside where the air is a fresher than the cave's. Smoke still rising from the rubble, now only faintly taints the air and the distance mutes the cries of scared children and grieving adults. A breeze carries the thick smoke-filled air away from the village, leaving streaks against the cold sky. If only we could wipe away our memories of the event as quickly as the breeze has cleared the smoke.

My family is among the lucky ones. Our home was untouched by the attack, but we will remain in the caves for a few days, so my parents are accessible to those who need them. I will be happy when I don't have to sleep on the hard ground or listen to mourning at night.

For several minutes, Rory and I have sat in silence, watching the activities below. I appreciate the silence. After the overwhelming noise from the night and the day before, I need to hear nothing. The tension within my scalp has released and my headache along with it.

Rory tosses a rock toward the edge of the viewpoint and we watch as it skips along the dirt before dropping over the edge, out of sight. There is no joy in throwing rocks today. Rory sighs beside me. "Did that boy tell you they would attack?" he asks. I assume this has been on his mind for some time.

"No. He didn't tell me anything. I wish he had said something. I could have warned everyone." My mind recalls the sight of the aircraft flying overhead and my dash toward the village. There was no time to warn anyone. My foot taps against the ground as my leg shakes. "I had no warning of what was happening until the aircraft came. He gave them a signal, and that was it."

Rory blinks and scratches the back of his head. "What kind of signal?"

"He had something in his ear. Like a radio. He told the aircraft to go."

"Why did he do that? Did you even get to talk?"

"We did. He made it about him meeting with the leaders. I thought he…" I don't even want to talk about him anymore. I was foolish to think he'd want to meet with the council. The boy used me, just like my father had warned. I gave them information, which they used to plan their attack.

"What happened?"

"He wanted to know if the leaders were meeting."

"And?"

"He asked if he could meet with the leaders and if they were meeting right then."

"Did he want to meet with them or not?"

I shake my head and stare at the ground. I don't want to look at my friend and see the disappointment on his face. He wanted me to talk to the adults earlier, and I didn't. He must believe this is my fault.

He leans forward toward the edge of the viewpoint.

"What is it?" I ask.

"I think they found someone," he says.

Now, I lean forward. A group of men have gathered around a burned-out structure. From here, it is impossible to make out the details. All I see are men surrounding the structure and standing on its top. They move quickly, clearing away debris. And then they stop. Some stand to the side. Others walk away. There are a few still working, but not as before. Whoever is in there hasn't survived, or they expect will die no matter how much of an effort they make.

"Are we supposed to sit back and watch the adults do all the work?" I say, leaning back. "Sure, we could cut ourselves on the metal or burn ourselves on the hotspots, but there are a lot of things around the village that could hurt us. They treat us like we're useless when we could be down there working."

"Have you asked?" Rory asks.

I shake my head. "What's the point?"

He shrugs his shoulders. "It's always worth a try. They're tired and we may be the only kids interested in helping."

That is true. I'm up here sulking and watching when I haven't even asked or offered to help.

"You're right," I say. "I will ask. Are you coming?" Rory nods his head.

I rise to my feet and we start down the path to find my father. If I want to help, I need to volunteer. I can't sit up here and complain like a child.

After much debate, my mother and the council finally agree to permit older children to volunteer with the clearing of debris. It is a fight to keep my emotions from showing when my father shares the news with me. Tears brim my eyes, and my throat tightens.

To protect my hands, my mother wraps them with cloth rags, making me the only volunteer with hands wrapped in fabric. Everyone else tackles the twisted metal and jagged pieces of snapped, burned wood with their bare hands. Soot and ash quickly blacken the once white cloth. Soon after, I tear them away, claiming they are preventing a tight grip. No one argues with my decision.

Following direction from the adults, I continue to move materials to the south side of the village. We place salvaged items in one pile and toss unusable debris to the side. There is more discarded material in the unusable pile than there is in the reusable pile, with more destroyed buildings to clear away. Hopefully, there will be more usable materials found.

Under the blistering sun, I tug on a sheet of metal, rocking it back and forth to free it from where it rests under a fallen beam. This piece was once someone's roof used to protect them from the elements. It couldn't, however, provide protection from an attack by the Nadeens.

Pressing the sheet against my side, my arms hold it in place as I carry it to the south side of the village. It is a good size and has only a few holes. They could reuse it when we construct new homes. Returning to the structure, I glance over to my father who has created a pile on the road. I assume that later he will focus on moving his items to the correct location, rather than moving each piece as he finds it. This may be more efficient.

Men shout from the next road over and my father drops a stack of wood to rush in their direction. Other men run from their positions. I look up at the sky. There are no aircraft. They aren't taking cover.

I follow.

They have assembled around a collapsed building. All are digging, except for one man who has his head and arms inside a hole. They aren't sorting the debris. The men throw wood and metal of any size toward the road or onto the collapsed building next door. They move swiftly and carefully. I hear a cry. The rubble is pinning someone underneath… still alive.

The mood has changed. People move with a sense of urgency, fueled by the excitement of finding a survivor. I watch the crowd of men digging and I feel my heart racing.

"Her legs are under there," I hear someone shout.

"Don't pull that," another yells.

From under the pile, a woman screams and the man in the hole moves deeper into the opening. He waves his arm behind him, signaling for the work to stop.

"She needs a minute," he calls out.

They pause. Rescuers support pieces of rubble to keep them from slipping back onto the victim. The man lifts his thumb, and the work resumes, but at a slower pace.

"Move that block over there," my father shouts. He points across the road. The men work to move a large section of an intact wall from the pile, easing it free inch-by-inch.

The man in the hole slides in deeper. His legs stick out of the collapsed structure. I step forward, wondering if he will disappear completely. The work continues with the pile slowly lowering. The man backs out of the hole and he waves his hand again, but no one sees him. I think I hear him yelling but can't make out his words over the noise of the men shouting orders and clearing debris. I run forward and kneel beside him.

"What is it?" I ask.

"Here," he says, passing a bundle of cloth. "Take him."

I look down at the bundle in my arms. A baby. His blankets are dirty. Soot coats his calm face. I brush my thumb against his cheek, leaving behind a smudge of ash. This baby survived. My throat tightens at the thought of such a little life almost being lost. He wouldn't have been the first. I have seen the small graves but holding him in my arms I am hit with relief.

Taking a breath clears away the tension in my throat and I regain control of my emotions. I must remain in control. I am surrounded by adult rescuers and I don't want them to see me as a crying child. I'm sure they aren't immune to the emotions of discovering someone alive... or maybe they are immune after years of managing their feelings.

"We have a baby," my father shouts. I look up at my father to see a wide smile across his face.

The woman howls from within the hole and my father refocuses his attention on stabilizing the debris.

"I've got a good visual of her leg," a man shouts from the top. "We can lift her out in a minute. Bring the stretcher."

Two men spring from the home and run down the road toward the caves, while the remaining men continue to create a clear opening to remove the woman from the wreckage.

The baby squeaks in my arms and I look down to see him stretch and yawn. Despite his ordeal, the baby appears uninjured and unfazed by what has happened. The medics will look him over and decide how healthy he is. I can only assume his mother shielded him from the collapse. It is what my mother would have done.

I place my finger against his palm, and his fingers curl around mine. He is strong.

"Hey there, little guy," I say to him. The baby blinks. "Your mommy will be out soon. Wait, a little longer." His lip quivers. "Oh. Don't cry. It's okay." I bounce him in my arms and rise to my feet. I have never held a baby before. With the men busy tending to his mother, I can't bother them to find out what to do with a crying baby. I keep bouncing him, hoping to remove the frown from his face.

It works. He blinks again and his face relaxes.

Having returned with a stretcher, the two men climb on top of the debris pile. The woman cries out, and the baby looks out the corner of his eye. He must recognize her voice. They lower the stretcher into the top of the rubble and soon rise with the woman strapped to the board. The men cheer.

"My baby," she shouts as they carry her toward the road. "Where is he?"

"I have him." I run to her side and tilt the wrapped baby toward her.

A rescuer holds out his arms. "I will take him with his mother to the caves. You can stay here with your father."

I slip my finger out of the baby's grip and hand him off. With the baby now out of my arms, I feel my pounding heart and shaking limbs. No doubt I am feeling the adrenaline from being involved in the rescue.

"Well done," my father says, gripping my shoulder. "I was happy to see you helping us out like that. I didn't even see Trav alert us he had the baby."

"I saw him waving and thought I might help," I say. My voice wavers and I clear my throat. "If I couldn't, I would have told you. I wasn't expecting him to hand me a baby."

"Well, you did a good job of taking care of the infant for us while we took care of his mother. Should we get back to work?"

With the rescue over, the men have returned to their original piles to resume the clearing away of debris. I wonder how many more people remain trapped under the weight of their homes, waiting for rescue, and how much time they have left before they will die? With so many homes left to clear, I am uncertain how the rescuers know which homes to search and which ones to leave alone. I'm sure they must know the names of people unaccounted for and they drew out a map, but what about those no one noticed were missing? I imagine it is impossible to keep track of everyone and their whereabouts at the time the Nadeens attacked. Not everyone would have been in their homes.

I push the thought from my mind and focus on the work ahead of me. Having removed another three pieces of reusable wood from my debris pile, I am proud of my work. It is challenging to move the large pieces out of the way, but I am satisfied knowing they can reuse some of what I have cleared.

A large sheet of metal stands in the middle of the pile, and I step on a charred support beam to give it a tug. This sheet will surely be useful in a rebuild. I firm my grip and lean back. The metal squeaks and grinds under the weight of a beam, but I keep pulling. Finally, it slides free, and I move it to the side. Among the blackened and broken debris, a fleshy color catches my eye. Draped over a wooden beam is an arm.

"Father!" I drop the metal and scramble over the debris. "I think I found someone."

"Colfar, wait." My father rushes toward me, his arms outstretched.

I peer over the beam. A man lies face-up, staring wide-eyed at the sky, his mouth ajar. He doesn't blink. He doesn't move.

My father pulls me back and kneels on the jagged pile. He holds the man's hand. Looking up at me, my father shakes his head. "I'm sorry you had to see this."

I close my eyes, but the image has already burned itself in my mind. It is the closest I have ever been to a dead body. I have seen them from a safe distance at the mouth of the caves, covered in blankets, but never still in the rubble. Never with pieces of shrapnel protruding from their skin.

I choke back tears and turn away, exhaling slowly. I don't want my father to think I'm weak. I breathe deeply and lift my chin. If he can do this, so can I.

My father pulls away the surrounding wood, watching carefully for what pieces may collapse inward. I step in to help, pulling boards away, placing them to the side. I hurry. I don't want to look at the man in the rubble any longer than I have to. Guilt twists at my stomach. I had been taking materials away while he was still inside his home. What if I have been stealing from him? I don't even want to continue to take materials from here.

"Aren't you going to call people to help us?" I ask.

"No," my father says. "Not when someone is dead. I'm sure they are also tending to other bodies out there. We will manage on our own and when it's time, we will call to have them help move him."

No one will gather around this building to remove the debris and this body. They won't dig quickly and shout orders. There is no rush when someone is already dead.

I toss a piece to the side, followed by another, and another. We need to move his body. It can't stay here. I pull on a piece of wood and the body moves, dipping to one side.

"Careful, Colfar." My father holds out his hand and places it on my arm. "You don't need to hurry. You can move slowly."

"Why? He's already dead. We won't hurt him."

"I know, but this is someone's loved one. We treat a body with respect and care, as if they were still alive. We do this for his family."

I want to forget that he is lying there staring up at the sky and work facing away from him, sliding more materials away and piling them to the side. Now that we know there is a body in this building, there is no moving of materials to the debris piles. We remain here until his body is free.

Once we have removed rubble from around the body, my father calls over another adult to help lift the man from the wreckage. Together, they wrap him in a blanket and carry him to the mouth of the cave while I remain behind to tend to the piles my father and I had collected. I sort their contents and take them to the unusable and reusable piles at the end of the village. My limbs feel heavy. My stomach churns. My head hurts. Why did I have to be one to find a body?

CHAPTER FOURTEEN

I stab my fork into the meat my mother has prepared for my dinner. Having no desire to eat, I stare at my food and push it around on the surface of my plate. I can't stop thinking about the man in the rubble. Was he dead long? If we had found him sooner, would he still be alive? Throughout the afternoon, I had considered asking my father what he thought, but I am afraid to ask, especially if working faster would have made a difference.

My chair squeaks under me as I adjust my position. Everything feels uncomfortable. I wonder if my mind is making my muscles ache or if it is merely a result of the day's physical demands. If I had an appetite, I could eat my dinner and excuse myself from the table. My mother will suspect something is wrong if I eat nothing, and I don't want her asking questions.

She sits down beside me and pulls her chair close to the table. "How did it go today?"

"I'm too tired to talk about it," I say, turning away from her.

If my mother can't see my face, she won't see the sadness I'm trying to hide. She always notices when I am upset.

"Your father said you were a big help today." She isn't saying she has noticed something is wrong, but I know she already has. It is why she is sitting here.

I shrug and drag my meat across my plate. Chatting with her will do nothing to loosen the knot that has formed in my throat.

"Are you sure you don't want to—"

"No. I don't want to talk." There it is. I knew her concern was coming.

Her eyes turn toward my father, who stares at me across the table. I look away. He knows what I saw. The man's body twisted around the beams of his destroyed home. I had disturbed his resting place. The ground where he took his last breath. My hands carried away the materials we salvaged from the pile after they removed his body. We robbed a dead man.

"I guess I should have told you," my father says to my mother. "He found someone today."

My mother leans forward. "What do you mean?"

"He found Lionel."

That was the man's name. Lionel.

My mother's right eyebrow rises as if she already knows what had happened to him. "Oh, Sweetie." Her hand reaches for mine. I pull it away.

"He died during the attack," my father says. "There was nothing Colfar or I could have done. He was most likely killed instantly." My father has fixed his gaze on my face. I'm sure his statement was for my benefit. It is clear he knows I am struggling, even though I am trying to be strong.

"Do you think letting the boys help was a good idea?" my

mother asks. "I'm thinking we made a poor decision letting Colfar go out there. Look at him. Maybe he shouldn't help tomorrow."

"This is real life, Ava," my father says. "If he doesn't see this now, there will come a day when he will."

"But he is so young. I don't want him to go." My mother wraps her arm around the back of my chair.

"I don't think we should make that decision," my father says. "I think we should leave that up to Colfar. It isn't as though we are training him to fight. If he feels he can go back out there, I think we should let him do it."

"I want to help," I say, clearing away the knot. "I want to do this."

"I think we need to let him." My father leans back in his chair. "The work isn't pleasant, but if today didn't scare him off, I think it's time."

My mother pushes back her chair. "No. I can't let him go out there again."

"Why not?" I shout, tossing my fork onto my plate. "All I do is sit around and wait for the adults to do all the work, or I fetch the things you ask for. I want to do more. I helped them with the baby today, but rather than talk about that, we're talking about him… Lionel. You want to focus on the dead guy and say I shouldn't help."

My father smiles. "You did an outstanding job with the baby. Everyone was talking about that."

"I didn't know you helped with him," my mother says. Her hand drifts from the back of the chair to my shoulder.

"I did. I saw Trav trying to get someone to help him at the pile. I went over and he handed me the baby. I didn't know what to do with him, but I talked to him so he wouldn't cry. That's about it."

"That was the right thing to do," my mother says.

"That baby's mother… Is she going to be alright?"

My mother holds my hand. "She is. And the baby will be fine, too. You did a wonderful job. I wish I had the words to express just how proud I am of all you've done today."

My father smiles. "You could give him some cake for dessert. That might show him how you feel."

She rises from the table. "That sounds like a wonderful idea."

"I don't feel like having cake," I say.

"Why is that?" my mother asks, turning back.

"Because… there are people in the cave who have nothing. The Nadeens destroyed their homes. They lost family members and I am in a house that is still intact, eating cake. That feels wrong."

My father nods to my mother, who continues toward the stove. "We need to take care of each other," he says. "People need us, but we can't feel guilty because our home is still standing. We are thankful we have our home and that we still have our lives. Over the next several days, we will cook in here to provide meals for others. Homes, like ours, will see lines of people outside their doors from people looking for help. Yes, they may live in the caves for now, but we can continue to provide for the people here. Tonight, you can eat some cake. Tomorrow, there will be plenty of work to do and more people who need our help."

I'd give my cake to someone else. I'd even give my bed to someone who is sleeping in the caves. I don't need it. I can sleep on the floor. We have so much that we don't really need. I have my parents and I don't need anything else.

With so many buildings leveled, there is little protection from the sun in the middle of the village. The volunteers work in the open as we continue to move the wreckage. Even after clearing away debris, two people are still unaccounted for. The council has delayed construction to focus on finding the missing. They assemble teams to sort through supplies and check over the reusable materials. Blacksmiths in the remaining shops work long hours preparing nails and tools. At the moment, no one is free to begin construction.

A bead of sweat dribbles down the side of my face. I can't remember the last time I worked this hard... if ever. No work I have done seems as meaningful as the work I do now. Everything else was a routine chore, such as delivering food to adults or watering plants in the gardens. This is something bigger than chores. I am contributing to the future of the village and the survival of others.

As quickly as I wipe away the sweat, another dribble forms. My mouth is dry, and any dust kicked up from the ground tries to coat my lungs. I don't know now if I am coughing from the dust or from the lingering smoke in the air. Regardless, it is choking me.

Through the corner of my eye, I see Corin walk up next to me. I haven't seen her since the attacks, when I guided her through the smoke toward the caves. Today, she is wearing a clean light-blue dress and stands beside me swaying back and forth, smiling. A canteen hangs over her shoulder.

"Hello, Colfar," she says sweetly. I have never heard this tone from her before.

I stifle a laugh. There is no way that dress of hers will stay clean long when dirt and ash surrounds her. Small flakes of ash still floating in the air have already speckled the fabric.

"What are you doing?" she asks.

Pulling on a charred support post, I refuse to allow her conversation to distract me. "I'm helping my father clear away the debris. You are welcome to help."

Her nose wrinkles. "I'd rather not. Is it hard work?"

"It is." It is a dumb question to ask, especially if she won't help. We need extra hands to clear everything away. We don't need onlookers. "How is your house? Was it hit?" I tighten my grip on the post.

"No," she says. "Our home is fine. They also spared our neighbors. We found everything was as we had left it. If you look inside, you would never even know they had attacked us."

Like me, they spared her home. Maybe she could lend a dress or two to girls who lost their belongings.

"How about your house?" She moves closer, looking at the pile of rubble.

I keep working and ignore her smothering. "My house is fine. There were quite a few homes that weren't hit. The Nadeens focused on the shops and the meeting hall."

"We were among the lucky ones, I guess." She slides the canteen's strap off her shoulder and holds it out toward me. "Here. This is for you."

I wipe away more sweat from my brow and continue tugging on the beam. "I'm fine, thanks."

"It's from your mom. She said you forgot it this morning." She dangles the canteen in front of her and waits, not accepting my refusal.

It looks like my canteen. I forgot to take it when I left home this morning. "Thanks," I say, taking it from her. I unscrew the cap and take a longer drink of water than I had intended. The water drips down my chin and pours out the corners of my mouth. Corin giggles as I wipe my arm across my face.

"You were pretty thirsty," she says.

"Perhaps." I screw the cap back on the canteen and toss it to the side for later.

"Did you want me to get you more?" Corin asks, strolling toward the canteen on the ground.

"No. There's enough in there."

"Are you sure?"

"I'm sure." I wish she'd stop offering to help. I can get water later and have work to do. If Rory and the other adults see her here, they will tease me. It is what always happens when the girls come around. If Corin talks at me all day, it will exhaust me and I have no interest in chit-chat, especially given what I uncovered yesterday. I imagine she would take off running if a body rolled out of the rubble and landed at her feet.

"What are you doing later?" she asks, returning to swaying back and forth.

"I can't think about later. I'm too focused on what I'm doing."

She laughs and plays with her hair. "You must have some plans. Are you going to be spending time with Rory and Hart when you're done?"

"Probably."

"Can I come?" she says, stepping forward.

"Probably not." The beam cracks and I adjust my footing.

Corin's eyes turn downward. She sighs and kicks at the dirt.

"I'd like to go with you. I always see you up at the viewpoint with them."

I ignore her and pull on the wedged post.

"Colfar." She takes another step forward. "Are you mad at me?"

"No. Why would I be?"

"I don't know," she says, slinking closer. "You don't seem to want to talk."

"I'm busy."

She crosses her arms and taps her foot on the ground. A cloud of dust plumes around her feet. "You could stop for a minute and talk, you know."

"No. I can't. The longer we take to clear this away, the longer it will be before we can build homes."

"Since when did you care so much about building houses?"

"I've always cared." Maybe not about building houses, but I care about the village and the people living here.

"I've never seen you care."

There's no point in arguing with her. All Corin has ever cared about is herself. Then again, I was the same way until I grew up. It was wrong of me to not listen to the adults. I had put my need to be useful above others and called it "helping". Not anymore. My focus is now on the work ahead and is more important than chatting with some girl. My father will be proud of me for making this work a priority.

I give the beam another pull and it hardly moves. I grunt and exhale, using all of my body to force it free.

"Let me help," Corin says. She rushes toward me. I feel my eyebrows rise. Corin has done nothing other than stand and watch. Now she wants to help?

She grabs hold of the post and together we pull backward. It moves an inch, then another, until it finally slides free, dropping any debris it had been supporting onto the rubble below.

"Thank you, Corin," I say reluctantly as I drag it toward the road.

She stares down at her soot-covered hands. Her nose wrinkles. "This is so gross," she says through her teeth.

"You could wipe them on your clothes," I say, smirking to myself. "That's what I do."

Her eyes widen. "On my dress?"

"Why not? Or you could leave it on your hands and help me carry this post to the salvage pile."

She shakes her head. Turning toward the road, she stomps away, all the while holding her hands out in front of her, away from her precious dress. I laugh. That will be all the help I will get from Corin. She was useful in getting the beam freed and she offered a distraction from the mundane work, but other than that, she was annoying.

"Hey, Colfar." Rory walks up beside me, carrying a reusable metal sheet. "It looks like Corin has taken a liking to you." As I had dreaded, Rory had seen her.

"I don't see why she'd like me," I say. The teasing has already started. "All I did was help her when the Nadeens attacked. She got a little disoriented in the smoke and I helped her to the caves."

"She's a girl. I hear they like that kind of thing. She has probably been all dramatic about it and told people you saved her life."

"Whatever." I pick up the post from the road and struggle to keep it off the ground as we walk side-by-side to the salvage pile.

"I didn't care that it was Corin when I helped her. I would have done it for anyone."

"I don't think that matters to her."

The post slips from my hands and slams to the ground. "Girls are stupid. They think everything is about them."

Rory laughs and readjusts the metal sheet tucked under his arm. "You saw how Corin was with Hart when his mother made him chop firewood for Corin's family while her father was sick. He helped for two days, and Corin followed him around for weeks. All Hart did was chop firewood. Imagine how bad it will be for you, now that you saved her life."

I sigh. Hart had complained incessantly about Corin's attention. Anywhere he went, she followed. We even tried to outrun her, but she still found him. All she wanted was to remain nearby to watch him and if she was lucky, talk to him. If he spoke to her, even in anger, her face would light up. It was both confusing and frustrating.

"I hope this is the end," I say. "Corin obsessed over him. I don't want the same for me."

"I'm afraid it has only just started. She will obsess over you for a long time."

I stare toward the caves. Corin could be obsessed with me for weeks… months… or even years. I hope someone else will come along and take her mind off me. I don't want her attention any longer than necessary.

My father smiles at me as I hand him his lunch. With the meeting hall damaged in the attacks, the council has opted to hold their meetings in the caves. I slink back toward the inner wall, and my father waves me off toward the mouth of the enclave. I know what that means. I am not invited to stay and listen this time.

Terrick moves to the center of the circle of men, and I slip behind the wall, stopping only to peek around the corner. Terrick takes a deep breath.

"It may concern us to proceed with negotiations after an attack," he says, "but we have little choice. The Nadeens have approached us with a ceasefire agreement, and it is an offer we must accept. While we won't receive any additional land, they will allow us to live here in peace, on the condition we request nothing else."

A man laughs loudly. "So, they're letting us live. They are so kind."

"It may seem like nothing," Terrick says, "but it is more than we had before. We have never had a ceasefire agreement. Obviously, Aldon's conversations have had some impact."

A feel a tingling in my limbs. Perhaps my conversation with the boy also got back to the Nadeens. It may have seemed like it wasn't effective, and the boy gave the signal for the strike, but they are now considering an agreement.

"The council has voted. Aldon, they have nominated you to attend the peace talks as the community's representative." My father looks at the ground and nods. Maybe he doesn't want to go. "You know the terms we originally laid out with the Nadeens and have established a relationship with them. As we discussed earlier, the Nadeens are also asking for you to attend. It makes sense to have you take part and might upset them if you aren't there."

"It is something I will need to discuss with my wife," my father says. His voice is quiet. If the walls of the caves hadn't carried his voice out of the enclave, I doubt I would have heard him. He isn't normally this quiet. "While I would like to agree to the results of the vote, I can't accept without first consulting with her."

"Of course," Terrick says. "I think none of us would expect you to decide without discussing it with Ava first."

"Shouldn't you be there, Terrick?" my father asks. "I think having two members of the council at the talks would be beneficial."

"If you think it would help," Terrick leans forward and grips my father's shoulder. "There might be something that comes up that requires some discussion, but I don't think all the council should go."

"I don't think so either. It would be unwise. If there is a problem, I would like a few of us to remain here to make sure the village continues to run smoothly and make any future decisions. I'd like one of those people to be Hayden."

"Alright. It is settled then," Terrick says. "If Ava agrees, Aldon and I will go with myself a few other volunteers to sign the ceasefire agreement. Hayden and the rest will remain behind. I expect there will be no issues, especially since we are giving the Nadeens everything they are asking for. They have left us with no other choice."

CHAPTER FIFTEEN

I pull back the blankets and climb between the cool sheets of my bed. It has been a long day of pondering what I overheard in the caves. My father told the council he would talk to my mother and she would decide if he could go to the peace talks or not. With me now in my bed, their conversation will most likely begin. As the adults of the family, they will decide what happens, but I would like for them to involve me in the conversation. I would like a say in if my father leaves the village to meet with the Nadeens.

"No," I hear my mother say from behind my bedroom curtain. "Absolutely not."

"But Ava—"

"No, Aldon," she says, cutting off my father. "I can't believe the council is stupid enough to consider it. The Nadeens just attacked. I'm still caring for the injured."

"I know," my father says. His voice is gentle. "But we have to. If we return to the Nadeens what was taken by Brocklund

Miller and we don't ask for additional land, they have agreed to no further attacks and will give us the land we have. We will finally have peace."

I sit up in my bed and turn my ear toward the curtain. The sheet of fabric is enough to muffle their conversation.

"There is something you're not telling me," my mother says. "I can hear it in your voice."

Whatever she heard, I didn't. I guess it is something that only a wife can tell.

My father sighs. "Tarsen, the Nadeen I have been speaking with, said their leadership feels we won't need to negotiate for more land now that we have fewer people." I cringe and my mother gasps. "I guess they feel they did enough damage to our community. They will probably try to make themselves look kind and generous in the eyes of their people by giving us this land." My father lets out another sigh that is longer than his last. "We can take this offer for now and try to negotiate again in a couple of years."

"How is sending you and Terrick to the peace talks going to help anything then? If they are offering an agreement with this kind of attitude, does it matter who goes?"

"They are asking for me and we will go in good faith."

"Good faith? After they attacked us?" My mother's voice cracks.

I lie back on my bed. It is rare for me to hear my parents argue. They are never this loud or emotional. I can visualize tears on my mother's cheeks and the redness of her face. Not only is she worried about what my father is saying, the care she has been giving to the community has exhausted her.

My father must feel the same. His face would frame his

warm eyes as he tries to console my mother. We have been working long hours in the village. I'm sure he would like to never need to search for bodies again, or clear away rubble. He could focus on building homes that could accommodate the growing families we have. The council could again focus on my suggestion of building homes vertically.

"Aldon, I'm worried," my mother says. "What if the Nadeens aren't telling the truth about their offer? I can't risk something happening to you."

"Nothing will happen," he says. "Tarsen has assured us that his people intend to sign the treaty."

"But what if they don't? What if you get there and everything falls apart? I don't like the thought of you being far away and running into trouble." Her voice trails off and is harder to hear. She must be at the far end of the room.

"It is a risk we need to take, Ava. It is for the community."

"Don't we do enough for the community?" she says loudly. "What about your family? We need you."

"I don't want to leave you behind either. If I don't go, then who should? Someone needs to represent us at the talks and out of everyone here, Terrick and I make the most sense. I hate to say it, but we are the most level-headed out of everyone. Plus, I am who the Nadeens have asked for."

My legs shake under my blankets, and my eyes tear. I'm certain the Nadeens asked for him because of me. Had I not told the boy about my father, they might not have focused on him. I have put my father in danger. I pull my cool blankets up to my hot cheeks and let them absorb my tears.

"Why would they ask for you?" my mother asks.

"They are asking for me because I am the one who has had

the most contact with them. I reached out to them about making a deal for more land. Terrick is coming because I asked him to."

"If that's why, then I understand," my mother says. "I still would prefer if you didn't go, though. It might be because I haven't been part of the conversations, but I am concerned that the Nadeens aren't being genuine."

"Tarsen assures me they are ready to make this the last attack, but we must do as they ask."

"Aldon, they have attacked us for years. I don't understand why they would suddenly be open to ending their strikes, especially when they just attacked us."

"The council discussed this point. The Nadeens want to negotiate while we are hurting," he says. "We assume the Nadeens want to do this when we will negotiate for our survival and nothing more. We'll take what we can get, and they know it."

"But what if you negotiate with them, you sign the treaty, and then they still attack us?"

"Again, that is a risk we have to take. If there will ever be a chance for peace on Elta, at some point we need to take risks. We have to try this. We have to make peace a reality on Elta."

It is quiet. I pull the blanket to my chest and turn my head to the side. Are they still talking? I stare at the curtain to my room. The light from the burning lantern flickers through the fabric and glows against the floor. They must still be in the next room if the lantern is still lit.

"But what about Colfar?" my mother finally asks.

"What about him?" I hear my father say.

"How are we going to tell him you are leaving?"

"I will talk to him."

Do they not suspect I am awake and listening? He doesn't need to tell me anything. I've heard it all. I only wish he would ask me what I want.

"When?" she asks. "You can't wait until you walk out the door. You need to tell him before that. There will be talk around the village soon enough. He'll pick up on it and won't be happy that he didn't hear it from you directly."

"Ava, don't worry," my father says. His voice is soothing. "I will tell him tomorrow."

"He won't like it. He will be afraid of what will happen. He will be afraid to lose you." I can hear the panic in her voice. These are her own fears, but she is right.

"There are many kids in this village who have no fathers or mothers because of this war. They could kill us in the next attack. What I'm doing will give more people a chance at a good life. I have always told Colfar that we need to give people chances and to look for the good in them. We need to give Tarsen a chance. From what I can tell, he wants to see this meeting happen, despite the negative messages they asked him to deliver. They don't have to offer us anything, but they are."

My mother sighs again. Her voice grows louder as her shadow grows along the floor and her silhouette appears on my bedroom curtain. "How much do you even know about him?"

"As much as I need to know to sign a ceasefire agreement," my father says. "His views are a little more progressive than some of their older council members."

"It sounds like they don't take his negotiations seriously, if they just attacked us."

"Ava, they have never offered us a ceasefire before. There could have been a disagreement in their ranks over how to handle this that may have led to this offer. We can't refuse the treaty because of what has happened. This could be our opportunity. We need peace. We need our people to be safe."

"Are you sure you want to do this?"

"I'm positive." Hearing my father's words, my skin feels cold and my stomach twists. I don't want him to leave. "In fact," my father says. "I have never felt so sure about anything before… except you."

"Oh, stop." My mother giggles.

Hearing my mother's laugh makes my cheeks rise to a smile. There is some remaining happiness in my home. Her silhouette moves away from the curtain and only the flickering from the lantern remains.

"I mean it," my father says. "I feel comfortable with this. If I didn't, I wouldn't be talking about going. I wouldn't ask others to come with me and put their lives at risk. Ava, you are everything to me. I don't want to hurt you. If you really don't want me to go, I won't. The council will find someone else, and I will stay here if that will make you happy."

Once again, it is quiet. She must be thinking… or they're kissing. Gross.

"Go," she says. "As much as I want you to stay, the village needs you. It is selfish of me to ask you to stay."

"It isn't selfish."

"It is. I don't want you to go because I'm afraid. I love you, Aldon. I can't imagine my life without you. I don't know what I'd do if—"

"I never tire of hearing how much you love me."

"And I never tire of saying it."

I pull my blanket over my ears and groan. As much as I am

happy to know they are in love, I don't need to listen to their romantic conversations. It does, however, make me hope that one day, I will be as happy as they are. I want to one day love someone who cares about me and my safety. Not right now, but one day far into the future. I'm not interested in talking to girls or obsessing over one, so there really is no point in thinking about marrying someone. In fact, it would surprise me if any of the girls here end up getting married. They aren't that bright, and they run away from anything that scares them, like spiders. If I find a girl to marry, I want her to be smart and brave. Someone who will stand up for herself and not get pushed around by the bullies in the village.

With the blankets snuggled around my head and my hands covering my ears, I close my eyes and think about what my future life could be like. Who would I marry? Corin? She has shown an interest in me, but she's too snobby to make me think I could ever like her in the same way as my father likes my mother. Corin never volunteers to help others. She is someone who needs help or runs from danger. I want someone who would stop running to help others. I don't want to say I want someone like my mother, but I want someone who shares the same values… someone who cares for people and looks for the best in them.

There are few girls in the village with those qualities… or at least they haven't shown it yet… or I haven't been around to see it. We're still young. Maybe when I'm older, it will become clear who I should be with. My father says people change and we should give them second chances. Still, I hope I don't end up with Corin. How crazy would that be? What would her mother think?

Tucked under my blankets, the warmth surrounds me, and I drift closer to sleep. My thoughts shift away from home until I picture myself running through the green, grass-covered fields above the village.

I'm not alone.

There is a girl with me. She's sweet. Kind. The fact that she is with me on the upper valley means she is brave. Already, she is a girl I might like to be around. Although I can't see her, I know she is there. I can hear her giggling. Her voice is soothing, like a song.

"Come this way," she calls.

I run toward her voice. I am laughing, running through the grass. I feel a joy and peace knowing she is there. Although there are Raven Snakes in the grass, I fear nothing. It is just me and the girl running through the field… at least, I think she is running with me. She is all around me, filling the air with her laughter.

"Where are you going?" she calls out again. There is more giggling.

I turn and run in the opposite direction. I must have run the wrong way. I want to run toward her, not away.

"Not that way, silly," she says. "Find me."

"I'm trying," I say. We must be playing a game. My eyes search the field. I see no one. There is nothing but green grass blowing in the breeze. "Where are you?"

"I can't tell you," she calls. "Keep looking. You'll find me…" Her voice fades.

My heart pounds in my chest. "Where are you going?"

"Just wait…"

She is gone.

I stop running and stand in the middle of the field. Alone.

When the girl left, so did the joy that existed when she was with me. Now, there is only wind whistling in my ears and the sound of footsteps. I turn. My mother is running up behind me.

"Colfar," she shouts. "Your father is gone."

"What do you mean he's gone?"

"He left to talk to the Nadeens."

I look toward the village. Smoke rises from the valley. Pillars of ash grow taller and fill the air above the village until the smoke hides the village from view.

"He didn't even say goodbye," I say as tears fall from my eyes. The smoke parts, allowing me to see my father in a distant field walking away from the village. Walking away from me. I reach out for him and call his name.

He doesn't stop.

Rain pours down from the sky that only moments ago was clear of clouds. I reach out again and try to run toward my father, but my legs won't move. Mud has trapped them. My arms ache as I hold them outstretched.

I take a breath and my eyes open. I am in my room with my arms lifted in the air. Cool sweat covers my forehead as my blankets have bound my legs. Sitting up, I wipe the sweat from my brow. My father hasn't left. He is still here in the house. My father wouldn't leave like that. He wouldn't leave without saying goodbye. I take a few moments to breathe, reminding myself that it was only a dream. Tomorrow, my father will tell me about his plans. For now, I need to put the thoughts of the treaty out of my mind.

I lie back with my head against my pillow and distract myself by thinking about the girl in my dream. The one who I couldn't find. The one I will find later and need to keep looking for. Who is she? Where is she? Why couldn't I recognize her voice?

Breakfast doesn't taste as good this morning. My father doesn't appear aware that I overheard his conversation with my mother last night. He devours his breakfast as if he is in a hurry, with no sign he intends to talk.

I sit across from him and pick at each piece of bread, waiting for him to strike up a conversation. I can't talk if I have food in my mouth, so I take only small bites. He scrapes his plate clean, and I realize he will leave the table without saying a word.

With his plate empty, he drinks a cup of juice from his mug and stares at the wall. Now, he is deep in thought. Maybe he isn't about to leave the table. I wish I could read his mind. Is he thinking about me and what he will say? Probably not. He has other things on his mind, like talking to the council and what will happen when he meets with the Nadeens.

I watch him lift his mug to his lips and take another sip. He stuffs a piece of bread into his mouth. His jaw shifts as he chews. My father even looks strong when he eats. No wonder the council wants to send him. He is one of the healthier people in the village. My father is also smart and, as he said last night, level-headed.

Now, I too am staring at the wall. There is nothing there to look at besides a small crack down the center of a wooden board. It is no cause for alarm. It is only a cosmetic defect but gives me something to look at. Staring at the walls, I notice how dark they are. I thought they were naturally this dark, but on closer examination, I see some charred edges. It was a few years ago when the Nadeens destroyed my home. Some boards must have been damaged and reused. I never noticed this until now. Perhaps it is because I am more aware of what happens after an attack than I was before.

I don't want to stare at a crack in a board. I'd prefer my father talk to me, but if he doesn't plan to say anything, I should leave him to talk to my mother in private. "Father," I say, continuing to look at the wall. "Would you mind if I went outside?"

He nods and I feel a wave of disappointment come over me. My father could talk now. I haven't left yet. He could ask me to stay and spend some time with him, but he doesn't.

I rise from the table, slowly pushing my chair back into place. I watch him. Aside from raising his mug to his lips, he doesn't move. His eyes remain focused on the wall. As I reach for the door handle, I turn back. "Do you think we could do something later?" I call to him.

He turns and smiles. "I'd like that." There are tears in his eyes I hadn't noticed before. I don't like to see him cry. In fact, I can't remember ever seeing him do so.

I run back to the table and wrap my arms around his neck.

"What is all this about?" he asks with a laugh.

"I heard you," I say, through my cracking voice. "I heard you and mother talking last night. I don't want you to go."

With my ear to his chest, I hear my father take a breath. His arms wrap tightly around me. "I know you don't want me to go. I'm sorry, Colfar. I won't be gone long."

"But what if something happens to you?" I sniffle. "It would be my fault."

"Your fault?" he asks, pulling us apart and wiping tears from my cheeks. "Why do you say that?"

"Because of what I told the Nadeen boy. I told him about you and Terrick being part of the council. They asked for you to go because of me."

He shakes his head and pulls me back into a hug. "Oh, no. That's not true, Colfar. They asked for me because I have been in contact with them for the negotiations. It is not because of you. You had nothing to do with their request. If anything happens, it is not on you. Do you understand that?"

I nod, but I'm not sure I believe it. I made a mistake and said things I shouldn't have. My father doesn't want me to feel guilty, but my stomach is already aching like before.

"I will only be gone for a few days. While I'm gone, I want you to go out and have fun with your friends. Especially, now. Put this out of your mind. There is nothing you can do to help except do as your mother asks while I'm away." He tightens his hug and releases me. "Go now and I will tell you more about when I am leaving once I know the details."

"Okay," I say, wiping the tears from my eyes. "If someone else can go, will you send them instead?"

"If there is someone else who can go, and the Nadeens will meet with them, I will stay."

I smile and walk back to the door. He waves and I slip outside. As the door closes, I see him turn to the wall. He is back to his own thoughts. Maybe he has also seen the crack in the wallboard?

CHAPTER SIXTEEN

The following morning, I hear my mother crying behind the curtain. I exit my room and she puts on a brave face, quickly wiping away the tears on her cheeks. The tightening in my stomach and the sickness I felt the day before continued to overwhelm me all night. My father is leaving today.

He crosses the room to place his hands against my mother's cheeks and gently kisses the top of her head. She wraps her arms tightly around him and cries against his chest. I have never seen her cry like this before. Even when surrounded by sick and injured people, she has been strong. This has weakened her in a way I never thought was possible. Today, sadness fills my home. It has been a place of joy and safety, but now there is fear. A fear that my father won't return home.

It is my turn to put on a brave face. My mother needs me to be strong and take care of things around the house. My father needs to know I will be on my best behavior while he is away. I will do my best to ensure my mother has no struggles. I will take care of her for him. I won't cry when he leaves. I show everyone I am proud of my father and he will feel comfort in knowing everything will be okay while he's gone.

And it will.

I know his daily routine for keeping the house running. I will chop firewood, should my mother need it. I will go to the market for her and gather our food. Any help she needs with cooking or cleaning up, I will do my part and his. My father doesn't have to worry. Everything will be fine here.

My father pulls the strap of his bag over his shoulder and takes my mother's hand, leading her toward the door. She gives her cheeks a final wipe and follows him outside.

People have already gathered, waiting for us to emerge. They have made a point of coming to send him off. Expressions of concern line their faces. One after the other, they shake my father's hand, thanking him for representing the community at the peace talks.

"I never thought this day would come," an older gentleman says, gripping my father's hand.

"Neither did I," my father replies.

A woman steps into his path and holds out a small loaf of bread. "It will be a long journey."

"Thank you." My father slips the bread into the top of his bag and continues through the crowd.

He shakes more hands, and they give more gifts. My father's bag bulges and overflow with food and warm clothes.

As a family, we walk to the far side of the village, followed by the crowd and stop beside the already assembled team. Someone has placed four supply bags along the side of the road, waiting for their departure. Four men will be going. Terrick stands with two others and waves to my father. They are ready to leave.

People with solemn faces and tear-stained cheeks say their goodbyes to the men. They hug and console each other. They are acting as if this is their last goodbye. It's not. I will see my father again.

I reach for my father's hand, giving it a squeeze. He kneels in front of me and grips my shoulders. "Colfar, I will be back as soon as I can," he whispers. "I know you will take care of your mother. You make me very proud, and I am so thankful that I can count on you. I will tell you everything when I get back."

I want to thank him for being a good father and teaching me what I know. I want to beg him to stay and tell him I am afraid, but I keep my words to myself and nod, sniffling back the tears.

"Come here," he says. He pulls me toward him and gives me the firmest and longest hug he has ever given me. In that moment, I realize that he also worries that he won't come home. This could be the last time he hugs me. He can't let go and neither can I. My fingers curl into his shirt, digging into his back. We say nothing as we hold each other.

Terrick places his hand on my father's shoulder. My father looks up. "It's time to go."

He nods and pulls away. I reach for him, but my mother holds me against her side.

I watch my father lean toward my mother, and above my head he gives her one last kiss. Rather than cover my eyes, I watch their public display of affection. My father steps back and as they part, I feel my mother pull me closer. My father will be gone for days. Until he returns, it will only be the two of us.

Walking over to the supply packs lining the road, my father

joins his bags together and pulls them over his shoulders. Fully equipped, the team reassembles and waves to the cheering crowd before taking their first steps away from the village. I am not in the mood for cheering. My father is walking away from me, just like in my dream. The wind will soon sweep away his footprints in the dirt. The further they walk, the smaller he appears, but I keep my eyes fixed on him, waiting for my father to look back. He doesn't glance back at me, or my mother. Should he turn back, he will see me being strong for him. I am not crying. I am holding my head high, swallowing away the lump of emotion in my throat.

My father stares straight ahead, walking alongside his teammates. He has a job to do. He is focused. He is leaving. I don't want him to go.

I break free from my mother and run forward, stopping just outside of the village.

"Father!" I shout. My voice doesn't carry over the void between us, and I am left with the image of his back as he walks away.

It has been three days.

The house is quiet without my father in it. I would almost describe the house as empty, but it's not. I am still here. My mother is still here. I miss waking up to the morning conversations between my parents. This morning, the sound of raindrops hitting the metal roof above me has replaced the sound of their voices. The rain intensifies, and the sound roars, drowning out the sound of my mother leaving her bed to prepare breakfast. I am alerted to her movements when a pot falls to the ground. I pull back my blankets, letting a chill hit my skin.

If my father was here, he would have already been up and to start the fire in the stove to warm the house while also heating the stove to cook breakfast. That is my job now.

I quickly slip into my day clothes and move into the main room of our house to find my mother chopping vegetables. My guess is she is already preparing food for the families in the community. The cool air makes my fingers numb and I rub my hands together before digging in the firebox for a bundle of firewood.

After I arrange bits of wood in the stove, I spark the fire with our family's block of flint. Coaxing a flame with my breath, it grows larger until it wraps around the smallest block of kindling. I smile as it crackles and sparks. Soon, the flames will heat the stove and I will be warm. I will also be able to eat.

"You got that fire started quickly," my mother says over her shoulder. "You're a good little fire starter."

"I watched Father do it many times."

"I am glad you watched him. Would you like me to cook you some oats this morning?"

"Yes, please." It will take time for breakfast to be ready. The stove will need to reach hot enough temperatures to heat a pot of water. My impatient stomach growls. It must wait to be satisfied. If my stomach wishes I would feed it earlier, it will need to wake me early.

A crack of thunder causes me to shift my gaze to the roof. "Do you think Father is in the storm, too?"

My mother sighs as she continues to chop the vegetables. "I would like to think he is far enough away from the village that the storm is nowhere near him. He is probably nice and dry where he is."

The rain pounds outside and my mind pictures my father huddled under a tree, with streaks of rain streaming down his cheeks. It must be miserable out in the cold storm with wind gusts directing sheets of rain toward vulnerable objects in its path. It will soak my father's clothes, along with any food or other supplies in his bags. He wouldn't have shelter, unless they raised a tarp over themselves, but given they had agreed to meet with the Nadeens in three days, the team won't have time to wait for the weather to clear. They must arrive at the designated site for the signing of the treaty to avoid offending the Nadeens or make them think the deal is off. My father is most likely walking in the storm… if the storm is over them at all. Hopefully, my mother is right, and the storm is nowhere near him.

Thinking of my father makes time move quickly and before I know it, she has finished cooking the oats. My mother scoops a serving into my bowl and my breakfast steams in front of me. Was my father able to eat a warm breakfast? They would have needed to stop and cook a meal over a fire. Most likely, he has been eating the bread and other foods given to him by the people in the village. They shouldn't have to stop other than to sleep. Still, it doesn't seem fair that I should eat a hot breakfast while my father is eating cold rolls. My father would tell me to eat the oats and not feel guilty and that I need my strength for helping my mother. I scoop a mouthful of hot oats into my mouth, although I refuse to enjoy it.

With a knock at the door, my mother steps away from the vegetables to find Ralda outside. She carries a cloth bag inside and shakes the rain from her clothes.

"My goodness. What a downpour," Ralda says, wiping her cheeks.

"What are you doing here?" my mother asks.

Ralda laughs and holds out the bag. "I've come with food. I also thought you might like a little company while Aldon is away. Since your family is sacrificing for our community, I don't want you two to wear yourselves out worrying. I know you well, Ava. Have you been sleeping?"

My mother gives a sheepish smile. "Not much."

Ralda places her hands to her hips. "Just what I suspected. And you think you will take care of the wounded and prepare meals when you haven't slept?" She shakes her head. "I won't have it. I had plenty of sleep last night. You will take it easy today and I will take care of you."

"Oh, Ralda. You don't have to—"

"I will not hear it," Ralda says. She points to a chair at the table and my mother follows her direction, taking a seat. "I'm also not going to let you send me back into that storm. I'm at least going to stay until the weather clears and you're just going to put up with me helping you in the meantime. Isn't that right, Colfar?"

With a spoon in my mouth, I can't reply and can merely nod.

My mother smiles and wipes her hands on her apron. "You're such a good friend, Ralda."

"And so are you, Ava. Now, what were you preparing over here?" Ralda asks, approaching the chopped vegetables.

"I was chopping some vegetables for the stew this afternoon."

"It would seem I came at the right time. You know I make the best stew."

She does, but I won't tell my mother that.

I loathe being outside. As soon as people see me, they ask questions about what is happening with my father away. I've only been outside for a few minutes to get some fresh air and someone is already on their way over.

"How is your mother?" an inquisitive woman asks.

"She is doing well," I say, scraping my muddied shoe over an embedded stone on the road. "My father will be home soon. Today is the day they will sign the agreement," I say, skipping to the topic that everyone wants to discuss when they see me.

"It is. We are all waiting to hear the good news." She clasps her hands together and smiles at me, as if I already know the results of the meeting and am keeping the news from her.

"I am waiting to hear, too," I say, causing her smile to dissolve. I have no news to share. "Although, I just want my father home."

"I'm sure you do." She looks about, now disengaged from our conversation.

"Do you think they're alright?" I ask. "Do you think the Nadeens will sign the agreement?"

"I would hate to think the men went all that way for nothing." She looks over her shoulder, as though someone had called her name. "I'd best be off. Tell your mother I stopped by."

It would disappoint my father to walk that distance only for the talks to fall through. For his sake, I want this to happen. I would hate to think what would happen to him out there if the talks were to break down.

For my village, I want the ceasefire signed. It has to be successful. I don't want to see my village attacked again. I don't want to have to help my father dig through debris to uncover bodies. I want to help him build homes for growing families. I want there to only be happiness in the village. I want to see the happiness I see in my home spread to the people in the community.

They are acting happy. There is an excitement over the team's pending return, and I can feel the sadness lifting from the surrounding people. There are smiles. People are hurrying through the streets with a renewed energy. A sense of hope.

We only need to wait a few more days for my father's return trip and the celebrations can begin. We will note this day in our history as the moment that there was peace between the Millers and the Nadeens. The day they signed the ceasefire. They will list my father's name among those who led us to this moment, and I couldn't be prouder.

My shoulders roll back. My chin lifts. My father will return a hero.

Everything will be better when he is home. Things will go back to normal. He will do his daily chores and I will have more time to myself. Under a treaty, if the Nadeens don't attack us, we can restore the village and then only build homes to accommodate growth. What will we do with our time when we no longer need to rebuild destroyed homes?

"Good morning, Colfar." A man waves from the door of his shop. "I have a gift for your mother." He disappears inside the building and comes out with a freshly carved, wooden serving bowl. "A thank you for allowing Aldon to travel to sign the treaty. I'm sure it has been hard for her to have him away."

I smile and thank him for the bowl. Over the last few days, the community has followed in Ralda's footsteps, expressing their gratitude through gifts and help with cooking and cleaning. My family isn't the only one receiving these offers. Generous donors have cared for all four families whose men have traveled for the peace talks.

Rather than feel thankful for their expression of kindness and appreciation, my muscles tighten from worry that the men won't return. As the day of their arrival draws near, the anticipation of hearing that my father is alright grows. I need people to express confidence in my father's mission and that the team will return with a signed treaty in their hands. I can't be the one reassuring them.

I look down at the empty, freshly carved bowl. It is beautiful with deep grains decorating its surface. My mother will enjoy the bowl… as long as there are good memories associated with it. I don't want this gift to remind her of something terrible. Of losing my father. I shake my head and push the negative thoughts from my mind. Waiting for news is hard.

Stepping inside my home, I find my mother and Ralda sitting at the table.

"You're back already," my mother says. She leans back in her chair and slides her hands onto her lap.

"A man asked me to bring you this," I say, passing her the serving bowl.

She turns it over and examines its shape. "It's lovely, but I really wish people would stop bringing us gifts. There are so many other people in need after losing so much."

Ralda smiles. "They want to do it, Ava. It is their way of thanking you and Aldon."

"But it should go to other families," she says. "We don't need it."

"Think of them," Ralda says. "They want to do something. Let them."

My mother places the bowl on the table and sighs. "I wish there was something we could do to encourage people to provide for the people here. I don't need a collection of supplies stored in my home when they could be useful to others."

"You're a good person, Ava. These people know you will use what they give you to help the community. You make meals. You care for people when they are sick. Everything they have given you is useful for what you do every day. These things will not go to waste by giving them to you, and you know it. This is the time for you to let the people take care of you."

My mother smiles and rotates the bowl with her fingers. "I guess you're right. As long as I can use it to help other people, then it isn't a problem."

Ralda rises from her chair and dusts off her hands. "Well, speaking of taking care of people, you and I best be going. We need to make our rounds to see how folks are healing."

They gather what bandage supplies we have left around our home, stuff them into bags, and step through the door.

I know, one day, I will also dedicate my life to caring for my community, but in a future filled with hope where there are no more attacks from the Nadeens.

CHAPTER SEVENTEEN

Two days later, I sink my plate into the soap-filled basin. It has felt strange to wash so few dishes these last few days. Soon, my father's dishes will be in the basin, adding to the work. I will be happy to clean them. My mother sits at the table mending one of my father's shirts. We have said little to each other all day. There isn't much to say. We're both waiting. My father will soon be here to add to the evening conversation. I've missed listening to my parents talk.

With the drying towel, I wipe away the water and soap residue before stacking the dishes on the table beside the stove. My father's dishes remain where I left them following his last breakfast here. My hand drifts to his cup and I slide my fingers along its rim. The house doesn't feel the same with him away. I can't remember a time when he left for so many nights in a row. I'm already missing the sound of his voice.

I replace the drying towel on its wall hanger and stand by my mother at the table.

"All finished," I say.

"Very good. Now, go get yourself dressed for bed. I will be in there in a minute to make sure you're tucked in."

She slips the needle into the shirt and pulls together the torn edge with the loop of thread. As he searched through the rubble, my father's clothes had snagged and ripped on the jagged edges of the debris. After my mother mends them, his clothes will look new.

I walk to my room and pull the curtain door closed before changing into my nightclothes and place my dirty clothes on the chair beside my bed. I climb under my blanket and listen for my mother to approach my room. She won't take long. My mother has learned the time I take to prepare for bed. She is never too early and never too late.

Sure enough, her fingers curl around the curtain and she pulls it aside to slip through. "All ready?" she asks, like she does every night.

I nod and smile as she sits on the edge of my bed.

"I wanted to tell you how proud I am of you," she says. Her eyes sparkle. "You have stepped up while your father has been away. I will tell him what a wonderful help you have been."

"You can't do everything when he isn't here," I say. "I had to help. I promised him I would."

She smiles. "You are right. And I am so very thankful you are my son and will make sure everything continues on as it should in his absence. People are saying good things about you helping around the village. You are continuing to clear away the rubble, I hear."

"Father taught me."

"He did, and you learned well. You are doing wonderful

work." Her face changes from a smile to sadness as her gaze drifts to the floor.

"What's wrong?"

She shakes her head. "Oh, it's nothing."

"But you look sad."

My mother reaches for my hand and holds it against her palm. "I am just hopeful that soon you and the other children in the village won't have to worry about helping with the adult chores. I am proud of the work you are doing, but I want you to have fun. To run and play."

"I have plenty of time to play. It's okay."

She gives my hand a squeeze. "Your father will be home soon," she says, as she pulls the blanket to my chin. "And when he returns, things will be different."

"Do you think the Nadeens will want to be our friends once they sign the treaty?" I think of the Nadeen boy by the hill. Would his attitude toward us change after a treaty is in place?

"I think one day they might be," my mother says. "It won't happen overnight. It will take time. We have been at war for a very long time."

"We didn't attack them, though."

"I know. However, their people believe they can't trust us and we deserve their attacks. It will take some time for them to replace those thoughts with new ones."

"When they become our friends, do you think their children will want to be friends with the kids here?"

Her smile returns. "Wouldn't that be nice? Your father and I have always dreamed of the day when the children on both sides could get along with each other. When that happens, there truly will be peace on Elta."

The sound of a knock at the door pulls her attention away from me. She looks over her shoulder. My mother turns back and leans in to give me a kiss on the forehead. "Sleep well. I will have a nice hot breakfast waiting for you in the morning."

"Goodnight."

She rises from my bed and pulls the curtain closed.

From my bed, I listen to the creaking as the door opens.

"Terrick," she says. "What are you—"

My heart rate rises. If Terrick is here, my father must be nearby. I sit up.

His boots tap as he crosses the floor. The door snaps shut.

"You look tired… or hungry," she says. "Can I get you something to eat?" Pans rattle. She is already busying herself with the dishes.

"No, Ava. I can't ask that of you." His voice is rushed.

"Then I should at least put something together for Aldon. I expect he will be hungry after a long journey." The banging of pans almost drowns out her words.

"Ava. Please, stop."

A pan falls to the floor. "Where is he?" she shouts.

"I'm sorry, Ava."

"Don't. Don't you say it." One of our wooden chairs scrapes against the floor and slams against the wall. I see my mother's silhouette at my curtain door. She tugs the curtain tighter across the pole. I close my eyes. I work to slow my breathing. "What am I supposed to tell him?" my mother whispers.

"Is he asleep?" Terrick asks. My mother says nothing. "Then we should keep our voices down."

"He's waiting for his father to come home. How am I going to tell him that his father is…" Her voice chokes, and she sobs.

He's what? The Nadeens signed the peace treaty, didn't they? The war is over. They will be our friends now.

I lie in bed listening to my mother's muffled sobs and strain to hear more. My father can't be dead. She would tell me if he were. How can I lie here and sleep when I can hear something has upset my mother and I know something has happened to my father? I pull back my blankets and my bare feet touch the icy floor, sending a chill up my legs. My heart beats wildly in my tightened chest. My legs shake and wobble beneath me.

Peeking through the curtain, I see Terrick's arms wrapped around my mother. She sobs into his shoulder. His hand gently rubs her back. My father is the only man I have seen hold her like that.

I push back the curtain and step toward them. "Mother? Are you okay?"

She takes a breath and wipes her tears onto her sleeve. Terrick takes a step back and lowers his hands to his side while my mother tucks her hair behind her ears and rushes toward me. "I'm fine, sweetie. It is late and you have chores to do in the morning."

"Is Terrick here because of Father?" I ask, half not-wanting her to reply.

My mother places her hand to her chest and turns away.

Terrick stands beside her. "I just returned and am here to make sure your mother is well. Others will do the same. You need to put yourself to bed. Tomorrow will be a busy day." His voice isn't as strong as I've heard it in the past. His voice sounds tight and weak.

"Tell me. Is he okay?" I say, pressing for information.

My mother crosses the room, moving further away. She

places her hand against the wall and faces the corner. She can't even look at me.

"Colfar," Terrick says. He steps forward and I take a step back. "You need to go back into your room—"

"No. Not until you tell me where my father is."

My mother's head droops forward, and she lets out a sob as she collapses to the floor.

Terrick grabs my shoulders. "Colfar, please. For your mother's sake. Go back to bed. I will tell you what has happened in the morning."

I look at my mother curled into a ball with her back to me. Her shoulders are rolled forward.

Terrick releases me and rushes across the room. "To bed," he shouts over his shoulder as he falls to his knees beside my mother. He places his hand on her back and she holds her face in her hands. "It will be okay, Ava," he says.

I slink back into my room and pull the curtain shut. My legs strike my bed and I fall onto the mattress where I lie, staring at the light under the curtain.

My mother's cries grow louder.

"We're all going to be here for you and Colfar," Terrick says.

I dig my fingers into my blankets. I don't want Terrick to be here. I want my father here. He was to sign the peace treaty. He was to make things different. My father is the only one who can make everything better.

Through the night, I have felt the weight of expected sleep pressing down on my limbs. My mind has worked steadily to blur the line between dreams and reality. But even though I wrapped myself in the warmth of my blankets, I never fully committed to sleep.

With the light streaming through the window, I know morning has arrived. My eyes are heavy and sore. It could be from the constant flow of tears that have soaked my pillow. My mother and Terrick did not admit to the death of my father, but I know what I heard. I saw the reaction from my mother. The image of her collapsing to the ground replayed repeatedly in my mind as I tried to sleep.

I lie in bed, thinking about getting up and starting the fire on the stove. My father said he was counting on me. I must get up. I roll over and pull back the blankets. Expecting the cold air hitting my skin, I take a breath. The temperature is warm. The fire must already be lit, which means my mother is awake and out of bed.

Quickly, I pull on my day clothes and pull back the curtain. Terrick is still here, sitting by the stove and stirring a pot. My mother sits on a chair in a dark corner of the room. She is wearing the same clothes as the day before. Someone has wrapped a shawl around her shoulders and draped a blanket over her knees.

"Good morning, Colfar," Terrick says from beside the stove. "Can I get you anything?" I shake my head. There is nothing he can give me. All I want is my father. "Why don't you have a seat at the table? I'll have your oatmeal ready for you in a minute."

I glance over at my mother. "She makes me breakfast."

"Your mother isn't feeling up to it this morning." Looking at the vacant expression on her face, I think he's right.

As suggested, I sit at the table. I place my hands in front of me and stare at my fingers. There are calluses on my hands from my work around the village. They aren't the same soft, child-like hands I had before. They are looking like a man's hands. I guess that's good, since it looks like I am the man of the house now.

Glancing up from the table, I spot the crack in the wallboard. I haven't looked at it since that morning with my father. Somehow the crack looks deeper, like it has split further down the board, but I'm sure it's the same as it was before. Whenever I look at the crack, I will think of my father and the last breakfast I shared with him.

"Here you go," Terrick says, sliding a bowl in front of me. "One bowl of oatmeal. That doesn't look too bad, does it?"

"Did you put sugar on it?" I ask. "My mother usually sprinkles the top with sugar."

"No. I, uh…"

My mother rises from her seat and rushes to the shelf where she retrieves the porcelain sugar container.

"Ava," Terrick says. "Let me."

"I've got it," she whispers. My mother unscrews the lid and holds the container over my bowl of oatmeal. Most mornings, she would use a spoon to sprinkle the sugar, but not today. She shakes the container over the bowl… and the sugar doesn't come. She taps the container and gives it a shake, freeing a large clump of sugar, which sinks itself into the oatmeal.

My mother gasps. "What have I done?" She replaces the lid on the container and sobs. "I've ruined it."

Terrick reaches for her shoulder.

"It's okay," I say, scooping out the clump and stirring in the remaining sugar. "I can still eat it."

"No." She shakes her head and continues to tighten the already secure lid. "That's too much sugar. It will be too sweet."

"It will be fine."

Terrick steps between us and takes the container from my mother. "Ava, he will manage."

"He can't manage!" she shouts. "We can't manage."

Terrick stares down at me with an encouraging smile and places the container of sugar on the table. My mother covers her face and turns away. I watch Terrick, once again, place his hand on her shoulder and I feel my temperature rise.

"I will take care of her," I say, pushing my chair away from the table.

"Don't worry about your mother," Terrick says. "Eat your oatmeal."

"No. I can take care of her." I push Terrick to the side and wrap my arm around my mother's waist to guide her to her chair. "We don't need you to take care of us." I say to Terrick. "We don't need you here."

My mother gasps and takes a step back. "Colfar. That isn't a nice thing to say."

"Father isn't here because Terrick and the council told him to go," I shout. "You didn't want him to go. I heard you tell Father you didn't think it was a good idea and he wouldn't have gone if the council didn't make him. It's their fault."

Terrick takes a slow breath. "Your father went because he believed the treaty could bring peace to Elta."

"Someone else could have gone," I say, facing him. "It didn't have to be him." I stomp my foot as I spit out my words. "Why do you get to live?"

"Don't speak to Terrick that way," my mother yells.

"It's alright, Ava," Terrick says, gradually lifting a hand. "He's just upset."

"No, it's not alright," my mother says, grabbing my arm. "Just because his father isn't here doesn't mean he can be disrespectful." She turns me around and pushes me away from the table. "Go to your room."

"But Mother—"

"Don't you argue with me." She continues to push me toward my room. "You will listen and sit on your bed where I want you to think about what you said." Her grip tightens around my arm as she pulls me to my bed. Tears have filled her eyes. "You will stay in here and won't come out until you're told."

"But—"

"No. I can't deal with this level of disrespect."

"I didn't mean to—" She is already behind the curtain. Her sobs have returned and mine have begun.

I grab my pillow and throw it against the wall. With my knees to my chin, I hug my legs against my chest. Tears soak my clothes. This isn't the future we had imagined. My father is dead and for the first time, she has sent me to my room without eating breakfast.

CHAPTER EIGHTEEN

For the next several minutes, I wipe my eyes and my nose against my knees. Snot and tears soak the fabric of my pants, and I recall the many times my mother has scolded me for wiping my nose on my clothing. Most occurrences have been on my sleeves or on the collar of my shirt when I have been sick. Today, it is the knees of my pants. I would use my handkerchief, but it is hanging near the stove to dry… or it was.

Dangling in front of my nose is my handkerchief, which I snatch out of Terrick's hand. As I wipe my eyes and nose, I watch him lift my pillow from the ground where I had thrown it and he carries it back to my bed.

"Try not to take it personally," he says, taking a seat on the edge of my bed. "Your mother is very upset and so are you."

I cover my face with my handkerchief and my lips quiver behind my fabric shield.

"She loves you, Colfar. She isn't angry with you."

"She is. You heard her."

"She needs space to cry."

I pull the handkerchief away. "Then give her some."

"I will," he whispers. "Ralda will be here shortly. I will leave then."

Ralda. She will be good to have here. Terrick can leave and then Ralda can take care of my mother. Terrick can't help us. He couldn't even help my father.

"Good," I say.

Terrick frowns and places his hands on his knees. "Colfar, why are you angry with me?"

"Because… you were the one who asked my father to go." My throat burns and cheeks grow hot.

"Where did you get that idea from?"

I push myself up on my bed. "I heard you. You told him the results of the council's vote. You didn't even volunteer yourself to go. You were just going to let my father go until he asked you to come with him."

His frown lessens, and his reassuring smile returns. "Colfar, that's not exactly how the—"

"I heard you. I was there. Behind the wall." His eyes shift toward the floor, and I twist my blankets around my hands, binding my anger. "You shouldn't have asked him. It should have been someone else that went. You didn't protect him out there. You asked him to go and you let him die."

Terrick leans back and clears his throat. "I'm sorry you feel that way. I would like to explain what happened, but I don't think now is the time."

"When will it be time? Everyone wants to wait to tell me things. Even my father wanted to wait to tell me he was leaving.

You didn't even bring his body home, did you?" Terrick shakes his head. "So, we can't bury him?"

"I'm afraid that won't be possible."

"Where is he? Did you leave him lying somewhere? Did you leave him where animals could find him?"

He reaches out toward me. "Colfar—"

I pull away. "Don't. Just leave me alone."

He doesn't say another word. Terrick rises from the end of my bed and slips behind the curtain. I didn't want to see him anyway. Terrick can go away and not come back.

Even if it looked like I had hurt his feelings, I was happy when he left my room. I am even happier that it has only taken a few more minutes for Ralda to arrive and for Terrick to walk out the door. What I'm not happy about is that my home is also full of people. Several women arrived with Ralda, and I have never seen my home this full before. Why have they chosen to visit us now? They should have been here when my father was alive. It is only after he is dead that they are here pretending to be helpful. How am I supposed to be with my mother when they all want to talk to her? They refer to themselves as a "distraction" from my father, but they are only distracting her from me. I want to be with her, too.

And then there is the food they bring. It doesn't taste like what my mother makes. The food is bland, and they use all the vegetables I don't like. They suppose their gestures of kindness will save my mother from having to do anything. It is their intent to allow her to rest and cry. Their contributions are only one more thing that makes our house not feel like my home anymore.

As a result, I hide out and become a hostage in my room. If I leave my private space to get a baked roll, the women will swarm me at the table. Each will want to comfort me in their own dramatic way. They have hugged me, cried over me, and lectured me on how to act after losing my father. I don't want their attention. I just want to get food because I'm hungry and don't want to sit on my bed anymore.

But here I sit. Afraid to leave my room because of well-intentioned people. I hope that my mother is finding some comfort in their company. All she does is cry while they console her, or they join her in crying. I wonder if it would be better for her if they left?

"He was such a good man," one woman says in the next room.

"He truly was," another replies.

A chair scrapes along the floor. "I think no one has checked on Colfar in a while." The voice belongs to Ralda. I lift my chin. "I will see if he needs anything," she says.

I need nothing besides food. I'd rather they leave me alone, but since it is Ralda…

"Colfar?" she calls from behind the curtain. "May I come in?"

I pull my shoulders back. "Whatever you want."

She slips around the curtain and sits on the chair beside my bed. "How are you doing in here?" she asks. I shrug my shoulders. "Did you want to stretch your legs outside?"

"Not really."

"I'm sure you would rather do something else than be inside and listen to a bunch of crying women."

"I want to be with my mom."

She rubs her hands on her skirt. "I can understand that, my dear. If this is where you want to be, that's perfectly alright. There is nothing wrong with getting a little fresh air, either. I hope we can get your mother to go outside, too. It would be good for her."

"What would be good for her is for everyone to leave her alone."

Ralda sighs and pivots in her seat to face me. "Colfar, we are letting your mother say what she needs. We have asked her if she would like us to leave and she has said she wants us to stay. Because of her, we're staying. What I want to know is, what you would like. Are you hungry?"

"Yes, but I'm not going out there."

"You don't have to. You can eat in here if you'd like."

"My mother doesn't let me eat on my bed."

"I have a feeling that she will let you today." She folds her hands on her lap and smiles. "What would you like me to make you?"

My stomach rumbles. It has been rumbling all morning. As long as what Ralda brings me tastes like my mother's cooking, she can bring me anything.

She leans forward. "I'm sure there must be something you'd like."

"Stew?" I look up at her.

Ralda leans back and laughs. "Oh, my dear. I can make you some stew. In fact, I will make enough for everyone. I will head down to the market to get some supplies and then I'll come right back here and cook you that stew."

Saliva whets my mouth. Already, I can picture a steaming bowl of stew in my hands.

"Do you want to come with me?" she asks, rising from her chair.

"No, thanks."

"Suit yourself," she says. "However, since I am cooking, I'd like you to do me a favor." I stare at her and blink. "Brush your hair before your meal. You need to be taking care of yourself, Colfar."

I nod and Ralda slips behind the curtain.

Looking back at the chair she was in, I wish she was still there. I pull my legs toward me and hug my knees. She will be gone for a while and even though people fill my house, once again, I feel alone.

In less than an hour, the house smells like stew. I close my eyes and breathe in slowly. The delicious scent of meat and vegetables fills my nostrils. Already, I can taste the flavors. The stew will be hot and will satisfy the pit in my stomach, if the pit is from hunger and not sadness.

The women with my mother haven't cried in a while. They could be hungry, too, and the smell of the stew may have distracted them. It doesn't really matter if they are crying or not. It only matters how my mother is doing. I slip off the edge of my bed and tiptoe to the wall to peek around the curtain.

My mother still sits at the table. One arm lies on her lap. Facing me, she rests her head against her other arm resting on the table. Dark circles have formed around her eyes. Her hair is a mess, with strands of hair loosened from the bun she had styled the day before. She still hasn't changed her clothes. She fixes her open eyes on nothing in particular. Blank-faced, she stares across the room. She doesn't look like she's aware of her surroundings. She looks… unwell.

With Ralda busy at the stove, the women have left my mother alone and talk to each other in two-person clusters around the room. One group sits at the opposite end of the table from my mother. They have turned their backs. Another group sits by the door. Have they given up on her already?

I haven't.

I slide the curtain across the rod, careful not to pull down too hard on the fabric, which would make the rod squeal. I step quietly into the room and my mother doesn't move. She stares straight at me, but it is as if she doesn't see me. No one else sees me either. Deeply involved in their conversations, the women take no notice of a boy crossing the room and to slide his arm across his mother's back.

"Mother?" I whisper in her ear. She groans. At least I know she hears me. "Are you okay?"

The room falls silent. Ralda turns from the stove. I stroke my mother's hair, hoping she will respond. Instead, she is staring through me. I've lost my father. I don't want to lose my mother, too.

Ralda waves one visitor over to the stove and hands her a spoon to continue stirring the stew. Ralda moves toward me, holding out her hand. "I think your mother needs a little quiet time."

"Why is she not talking?"

"She hasn't slept," Ralda says, wrapping her arm around me. "Come with me to get some extra wood for the stove. I will need your strong arms to carry the wood inside."

"But I want to be with—"

"Come along, Colfar. The fresh air will be good for you."

There is no arguing with Ralda. She leads me outside where the bright sunlight stings my eyes. Having spent many hours crying in my dimly lit home, I raise my arm to my forehead to create some shade and shield my eyes.

"There's some wood over here," Ralda says.

Already, she has pulled two pieces of chopped firewood from the stack. Two pieces I had helped my father add to the woodpile. I watched him cut each piece, moving out of the way as the wood few through the air under the power of his axe. I will never watch him chop firewood again.

"Hold out your arms."

I stare at the pile. Soon, we will deplete the wood until there is nothing left. Will my memories of him fade, too?

"Colfar, what's wrong?"

Who will chop the wood now? The chore will land on me, no doubt. All of my father's chores will be mine. My mother had said everything would be different when he came home. She never said how things would be different if he didn't.

Ralda pokes my chest with a log. "Wake up, Colfar. We have work to do."

I shake my head. I don't want to work. I don't want to do anything. I just want to cry... but not here. Not where everyone can see me.

My eyes scan the village. The roads are mostly empty. People are inside their homes, unaware I have stepped outside and am fighting back tears.

Ralda returns the firewood to the stack and wraps her arms around me. "You need a hug, don't you?"

I nod against her chest. A tear pools in the corner of my eye. I wipe it away and another quickly follows. She rocks me back and forth. For a moment, the warmth of her hug makes me feel safe.

I let the tears fall.

"You don't need to do any work if you don't want to."

"I need to," I squeak. "My mother needs help. I promised my father."

"You need to rest." Her voice sounds muffled, vibrating through her chest.

"No, I don't. I'm fine." I push her back and wipe the tears from my eyes.

"Colfar, don't do anything right now other than what feels right to you."

Ralda looks at me with her friendly eyes. While they look sadder than usual, I can see that she cares and is doing for me what my mother can't right now.

"I don't want to push you, Colfar, but I don't want you sitting inside in the dark with your mother when she isn't well. Is there anyone you would sit with? Talk to?" I shake my head. "How about Rory?"

"Rory hasn't been by since…" Since before we got the news from Terrick. Rory was helping me clear away debris. Normally, he would have come by to walk with me to the worksite. He hasn't come by. He has left me, too, in his own way.

"Rory may have thought you would want to be left alone. If you were to find him, he'd probably be thrilled to see you."

"And do what? Play?" I grind my foot against the ground. What a suggestion. I can never play again, not after losing my father. I am a man now. Men don't play.

"If you want," she says.

I don't want to. "What would people think if I was outside playing and having fun after this? Why should I play when my mother is inside the house crying? I can't be playing with my friends. Not now."

"If not now, when?"

When? Will there be a time when I can play with my friends again? My father is dead. It is time for me to grow up and work. I must clear debris and help construct houses. There won't be time to play with Rory and Hart. I can't throw rocks onto the rooftops of the village. I have too many responsibilities now.

"Never," I say. "Life is different now."

"Oh, my dear." She wraps her arms around me again. "Your father would want you to still live your life. He went to sign the agreement so you could be a child. He wanted to see you play. Don't let his death keep you from living. Let his life inspire you to do more. To be more. That means, enjoy the life your father fought so hard for you to have."

The village is what my father died to protect. The village and the people living inside it. I imagine the streets being empty, with everyone giving up and shutting themselves away. The village wouldn't be the same place anymore. It would be sad and a depressing place to live. My father died so people could have joy and hope. Not the opposite.

"Show the people what it looks like to live, Colfar," Ralda says. "Show your mother you will be okay."

I take a breath and step out of Ralda's embrace. I don't know if I will be okay. I don't know how long it will take for the tears to stop falling or for me to feel comfortable enough to play. For now, I will do as she says. I will show people what my father wanted. I will help them continue to be the village he died trying to save.

I hold out my arms. "I'll carry that firewood now."

CHAPTER NINETEEN

Five days later, Ralda hands me a list of items to retrieve at the market. Remembering the promise I made to myself to help the village and be well for my mother, I take Ralda's list and set out across the village. People whisper and stare as I walk by. I do my best not to notice them and keep my head down, focusing on the dirt road in front of me.

Ralda says my mother should return to her old self soon, but I worry that she won't. She and my father were happy when they were together. With him gone, I wonder if I alone will be enough to make her smile. So far, I haven't been.

With Ralda's encouragement, my mother has since changed her clothes and is eating again. Every once in a while, she says a few words and is most animated when sharing a favorite memory of my father… and then she cries again. It is as though she won't allow herself to be happy, even for a moment.

Having seen a few glimpses of life in my mother, I am growing increasingly comfortable with my choice to leave the house. I give myself permission to be among people and return to the routines of before, even when I can't imagine continuing on without my father. Rory has been by and we go for walks together with Hart, but there has been no playing. Not yet, anyway. We just walk and talk about what they have been doing.

It feels strangely good to be at the market today. While nothing feels normal, doing something familiar makes me feel that, to some small degree, things will eventually be okay. I compare the food in the basket to the items on Ralda's list. Being at the market and gathering supplies at least makes me feel like I am being helpful to Ralda and the food I get will help to feed my mother… if she continues to eat what we put in front of her.

With the items gathered, the man in charge of the market adds their names to the ledger.

"Are these for your family?" he asks.

My family? It is only my mother and I now. Are two people a family?

"Ralda said to add it all under her name," I say.

"I've already noted it under yours. Ralda can take it up with me if she needs it changed."

I nod and dump the supplies into a cloth sack to bring home. Luckily, the vegetables aren't that heavy, and I sling the bag over my shoulder before I start down the road.

"Colfar, wait," I hear from behind me. Terrick tugs at my sleeve.

I pull my arm free and take a step back. "Let go."

"I need to talk to you," he says with sunken eyes. Now, Terrick doesn't look well.

"I don't want to talk." I hold my bag of vegetables tight against my shoulder.

"Colfar, I only want to help."

He wants to help me? Does he feel guilty about what happened? He knows what he did or didn't do out there. For all I know, my father's death could have been Terrick's fault and now he wants to make it better. I won't let him.

Terrick sighs. "I came by the house to check on you and your mother. Ralda said you would be here."

He checked on my mother? Did he try to hug her like he did the night he told her what happened to my father? He can't step into the hole my father has left behind. He can't comfort my mother. She needs my father. He loved her. Terrick can stay away from her and away from me.

"Leave my mother alone!" I shout. "Just because my father is dead, doesn't mean you can have her."

Terrick shakes his head. "Colfar, I am not trying to take your father's place and I have no intentions toward your mother. She needs support, and so do you."

"I don't need your support. And my mother has me to take care of her. She doesn't need you."

He doesn't move. He doesn't turn away. Terrick looks at me straight on and attempts to smile. "You're right. She has you. And, she has Ralda. But she needs to ask me questions about what happened, and I need to be available to answer them. Sometimes adults need to talk with other adults. Your mother won't want to burden you with her questions."

"Well, she should. I'm her son."

"And you are a child."

"One minute people tell me I'm a child and the next they tell me I'm the man of the house. Which is it? Am I a man or a child?"

"Which do you want to be?"

What does he mean by that? Which do I want to be? I know how I want them to treat me, but I don't want all the responsibilities of a man. Not yet. "I want to be a man someday."

"But not today?"

I shake my head.

"Then don't be. Be a child, Colfar. You have permission to be a child a while longer. This war has forced many children to grow up fast, and you don't need to. We will help your mother and you." My head hurts and so does my throat. I won't cry in front of him. "I want to help you, Colfar. I want to be here for you; however you need me. For now, why don't we get those vegetables to Ralda?"

Every meal without my father is a reminder he is dead. He'll never wear his freshly mended clothes that my mother has left draped over the chair at the table. He's just gone. Many items he last touched remain where he placed them. Things like his spare hat that sits on a shelf near the stove. His favorite hammer propped against the wall beside the door. We have left them there where they will collect dust.

I hold his mug and turn it over in my hands. It feels lighter than I remember. Perhaps that is because I always carried it to him full of tea or water. My fingers curl around the handle and then slide back to the rim. There isn't even a stain at the bottom of the cup. No evidence he used to drink from it.

"What are you doing?" My mother's voice startles me. My hands shake and the cup slips. Helplessly, my fingers flail in the air, searching for the mug as it tumbles toward the ground and shatters on the floor.

My mother gasps, and I fall to my knees. Fragments of various sizes litter the floor. Some pieces have slipped between the floorboards. Other shards fell by the wall. I frantically grab at fragments of porcelain. I brush my hands against the wood and push together what pieces I can. But there are too many. It will be impossible to repair.

"I'm sorry." My eyes pool with tears. "I didn't mean to drop it."

"That was your father's!" my mother shouts, kneeling beside me, collecting the shards of porcelain.

"I only wanted to hold it."

"Why? Why would you do that?" Holding out her apron, she cradles the broken pieces in the fabric.

"I didn't want to break it." Tears blur my vision. The fragments are invisible now. "I just wanted to hold something that belonged to him."

"You shouldn't touch his things. They aren't yours." She pushes herself off the floor and piles the pieces on the table. Laying each piece out, she examines the shapes and attempts to fix the fragments together. "I can't believe you were so irresponsible. Of all the things for you to have done—"

"I said I was sorry," I shout, rising to my feet. "Why don't you just send me to my room? It isn't as if you want to talk to me anyway. Or I could go outside. You probably don't even want me in the house with you."

I stomp across the room and swing open the front door.

"Colfar," I hear her call from behind me. Ignoring her, I let the door slam and I continue down the road.

She can be mad at me. I'm mad at her. I didn't mean to break the cup. It was as special to me as it was to her. Yes, the mug wasn't mine, but my father was. If I want to look at something that reminds me of him, I should be able to.

It was her fault it broke. She startled me. That is how it fell. Now, we can't replace it. The cup is gone, just like my father.

While my mother is still here, it feels like she isn't. She doesn't smile like before. She no longer hugs me. We rarely talk. Still, I want her to know that I need her. I can't lose her to sadness. She is all I have left of my family. If she couldn't imagine what her life could look like without my father, I need her to understand that I can't imagine my life without her. How am I supposed to deal with losing both of my parents? Also gone are her routines of making me breakfast in the morning and saying she is proud of me. Now, I am a disappointment. I am irresponsible. Does she even love me anymore?

Ralda has assured me she does. That my mother is only grieving my father and can't see beyond her own sadness. I want my mother to see me. I want to make her happy. It would make me happy to see glimpses of what my life was like before my father died. To have a moment or two of happiness. If only my mother could spare a few minutes away from her grief to live life with me.

Ahead of me on the road, I see Marlow walking alone. I understand him now. Having lost both parents in an instant, he knows what it is like for life to change. Marlow is angry and I feel that way myself… especially toward Terrick.

"Marlow," I call out to him.

He turns. I pick up my pace until I stand beside him.

"I'm sorry about your father," he says. I nod. The lump in my throat has returned. "Is your mother doing, okay?"

"No. We just had a fight. I dropped my father's cup this morning, and it broke."

"That's too bad." He looks down the road and shoves his hands in his pockets. "I was going to find my brother and a few of the guys to see if they wanted to play a game of Tusselball. Did you want to join us?"

Is this happening? The boy who used to knock me to the ground now stands beside me with kinder eyes. We extinguished the fire on the bridge together. We had to clean the market as a consequence for our fighting. Now, it seems we have a deeper understanding of each other. We both have experienced the loss of loved ones. Perhaps I can learn something from him about how to move forward. He could show me how someone can carry on after they lose a parent. Or in his case, both.

With a nod of my head, I follow him down the road and for the first time since the day I learned my father died, I play.

For two hours, we play Tusselball with Rory, Hart and other kids from the village. Our teams tackle each other, and we throw our opponents to the ground for possession of the ball. I will have bruises from the hard landings and tackles. I fill my lungs with oxygen and feel alive. For once, I don't feel guilty for feeling this way. I need to spend more time with my friends. I need to be active, doing things such as building homes. This is what Ralda has been encouraging me to do. I wish I had done this sooner, but I wasn't ready. This was the right time. I guess I have Marlow to thank for inviting me.

One by one, we shake hands to congratulate each other on a great match. Everyone is smiling, even me, and it makes my cheeks hurt. After only a few days, my facial muscles have been out of practice. Marlow and his friends walk away, leaving Rory, Hart and me in the field. I don't want to go back home yet. I want this breathing room of happiness to last a little while longer.

"Is that Terrick?" Hart asks, pointing to the end of the field.

Hart is right. Terrick leans against a blossom tree, watching us in the field.

"What do you think he's doing here?" Rory asks.

"Who knows?" Hart shrugs.

My guess is Terrick has come for me. Since he has come by the house regularly, I have little doubt he has come here after a visit to my home.

We cross the field and Terrick gives Rory and Hart a wave as they walk by. As I approach, he steps away from the tree.

"I've come from seeing your mother," he says. My guess was correct. "She said that the two of you had a disagreement?"

"I wouldn't call it a disagreement," I say. "I accidentally broke my father's mug, and she was mad at me."

"She isn't angry with you, Colfar. In fact, she feels terrible about what happened."

"She does?"

He points toward a log and a rock at the side of the field. He takes a seat on the rock and I sit on the log across from him.

"It upset your mother to have lost something that reminds her of your father." Terrick sits upright. He looks like his health has recovered and is back to being as confident as I've seen him in the council meetings. "Every little item that belonged to your father is important to her. It was the emotion of losing the cup that made her upset. She understands why you wanted to hold it… because she has been holding it, too."

"She has?" I haven't seen her with it. The most I've seen is her standing beside his mended clothes on the chair while she stares at them.

"When you are asleep," Terrick says, followed by a sigh. "Listen, Colfar. Your mother and father were together for a long time. Since they were children, really. I still remember when your father told me your mother had caught his eye. There was no turning back for him after that. His loss will hurt your mother for a long time. Your father was special to your family and to the community, and we all miss him."

I look past Terrick, toward the buildings. A thin layer of smoke from burning stoves, and still smoldering rubble, settles over the remaining rooftops. My father died for this village and the people in it. He sacrificed himself to bring people a future.

I fight back tears with my growing sense of pride. My father was special to the people here, and he saw something special in this place. I see it, too. This community, nestled between the valley walls, is my home. The people have cared for my mother and me after losing my father. They are my family, and I would do anything for my family. I might even be willing to die for them, as my father did.

"Your mother would like me to bring you home," Terrick says.

"I was planning to go home soon."

"How about now? She would like to apologize to you for

what happened earlier."

"She doesn't have to," I say. "But I understand." My mother had yelled at me and it hurt. She has said so little over the last few days and these were the first coherent words she had spoken. They weren't to tell me she loved me or that she was proud of me. She said I was irresponsible. Is that how she feels about my father? Was he irresponsible for going to the sign the treaty?

"Colfar," Terrick leans forward. "Before we go, I have something to ask you. I have already spoken with your mother, and she has agreed."

I adjust my position on the log. He has my attention. "Agreed to what?"

Terrick smiles and takes a breath. "Your father and I were good friends throughout our childhood. Just like how Rory and Hart have been to you. I know that your father had intended to teach you what you would need to know to take care of this place."

"What do you mean?"

"I mean, he would have wanted to teach you more about how the council operates, understand the crops, how much we need to produce to feed people, how to shoot a rifle, and how to lead. He wanted you to learn these things because he felt you had the potential to lead the next generation. I believe that as well. We need to invest in you and in others like you."

I scratch my forehead. This is what I wanted to learn from my father… and he wanted to teach me. With him gone, who will—

"Colfar, I would like to take this on. Your father would want you to learn these things, and I feel he would be pleased if I stepped up to do this for you."

"You want to teach me?"

"Yes. I would like to teach you what I know… if that's alright with you."

Only days before, I hated this man because of what happened to my father. I blamed him, but he hasn't let that stop him from caring for his friend's son. He is still here after what I said and how I treated him. My father isn't here, but Terrick is. My father wanted this, and I will do it for him. I will learn all I can to help the community he loved.

"I'd like that," I say.

Terrick leans back, and his smile widens. "There is a lot to learn, Colfar. I can see the man you will become. I saw it during the attack. You were braver than many of the adults that day. You risked your life to extinguish the fires on the bridge. That alone showed me your leadership potential." My heart beats faster. Terrick, the leader of our village, is proud of me. "Now, we should get going to see your mother. I'm sure she will be happy to see you."

We set off together down the road as mentor and mentee. I am excited to tell my mother what I have discussed with Terrick. I may even share with her about playing Tusselball with Marlow. Instead of my life changing for the worse, this feels like a new beginning.

At the house, I find Ralda already visiting. My mother greets me with a hug and apologizes for her earlier outrage. While things aren't the same with my father gone, we still have each other. Wrapped in her arms, I hear her heart beating and I feel her comfort. I look up at her face and for the first time in days I see her smile. My mother will be okay and so will my community.

EPILOGUE

I dip my hands in the basin and splash cool water over my stubble-covered face. Much has changed in the twelve years that have passed since my father died. No longer am I that eleven-year-old boy. I am a grown man now and share a home with other single men in the village. This morning, I am the last to leave, but for good reason. I am moments away from leaving the village to travel with a team to sign a peace treaty with the Nadeens.

I smile as I run my hand along my jaw. We are not naïve and are leaving fully prepared for the Nadeens to betray us as they had when my father died. How appropriate would it be for me to die in the same way? I will not die full of trust. I don't trust them, but I will take the risk. As my father had said, there can't be peace on Elta unless we take risks.

Gently, I glide the blade over my cheek, scraping away the rough hairs and leaving a smooth strip of skin. It will be days until I can shave again. How I long for the days when my face was soft, and I didn't need to spend my mornings grooming. Again, I smile. I'm fooling myself if I think those days were simpler. Life has never been simple.

Another splash from the basin and I rinse away the cut hairs that have stuck to my skin. With a last pat of a towel, I feel refreshed. I'm almost ready to leave. I glance at my packed bag lying on my bed and my stomach twists. It is all too real. I am leaving this place. I jump at the sound of someone banging at my door. Hopefully, I am more courageous when I meet with the Nadeens.

Opening the door, I find Rory and Hart, both standing with their packs strapped to their backs.

"Ready to go?" Rory asks.

"I am."

If only they were here to invite me to go play or run up to the viewpoint like the old days. All three of us are on the team together. We will represent our community at the peace talks. While I am to lead the team, I can't imagine making this journey without them.

I throw my pack over my shoulder and close the door behind me. The gravel crunches under my feet. For the next several days, I will walk to the Great Plateau to meet with the Nadeens. I won't have the comforts of home, unless I count my friends by my side.

"I am lucky I could shave this morning," Hart says as he runs the palm of his hand over his cheek. "With the way my hands were shaking, I thought I would cut myself."

"Same here," I say. It would be ridiculous of me to deny how I was feeling. My stomach has been tight all night, making my insides ache. I have hardly slept, and my eyes burn in the bright morning light. But there is no time to complain. "We should get moving. They will be waiting."

Our teammates and the entire community have waited weeks for this morning to arrive. Just like the day my father left, they line the roads to wish us well. Many people shake our hands and slow our procession toward the entrance to the village where Terrick and the rest of the council wait with our team. We are all hopeful that this time the war will end, and peace will begin. We have waited so long.

Terrick smiles and shakes my hand. "I'm proud of you, Colfar. You will lead them well."

"I hope so," I say. I'm not so sure I can. Some of these men are older than me and have already voiced that someone as young as me shouldn't be leading them. Even after their complaints, none of them volunteered to lead and so I still carried the weight of the responsibility. I feel ill-prepared.

"Remember what I told you," Terrick said. "Put your men first."

I can do that. My parents modeled that throughout my childhood. I will do what I have to and make sure we return. I can't let their families live through what I did. They can't lose their loved ones and not be able to bury them.

"I am confident you will represent our community well at the peace talks. There shouldn't be anything for you to do other than sign and shake their hands. Everything should be settled."

"I hope you're right."

"If I'm not, all of you are armed and can defend yourselves if needed."

He opens his mouth, as if to speak again and pulls me into a hug. It is a tight embrace. He hasn't said it, but I know this worries him. Our friendship has evolved and grown over the years. Terrick has become more of a father to me than I ever imagined. He has challenged me to work harder and be a better man. He has given me opportunities to gain influence within the community and show my potential.

People no longer see me as the young boy who would get into mischief and fight with Marlow. They see me as a man who works long hours to serve his community and tell me I am the spitting image of my father. I like to believe they see both my father and Terrick in my actions. Both men have influenced me, equally.

I am thankful for what Terrick has taught me. He has inspired me through his leadership in the community and with the council. He has taught me about self-sacrifice and putting the needs of the community above my own. He shares the same love of the village as my father did. His friendship and caring have given me the confidence to push myself further and gain a greater understanding of myself. I know what I am capable of and that when I think I have reached my limit, I can always do more. I am thankful that he stepped up and taught me what he has. I have learned much about leadership from him. It still hurts when I think about the day my father died but am thankful for the man who has taken me in as his own, especially when that wasn't the end of the losses I would experience.

"Your parents would be proud of you." Terrick gives me a last pat on the back.

They would be proud of me. My mother told me that many times over the five years after my father's death. I loved hearing those words from her. She spoke them the day before she died. As she had done many times before during an attack, she ran to help the injured only for a Nadeen aircraft to strike her down. I held her in my arms as she took her last breath. On that day, I lost the last member of my family and my home. For a time, I thought I wouldn't recover from the loss of my mother, but Ralda stepped into the void my mother left behind.

Today, she does the same.

"My boy," she says, bumping Terrick out of the way. She wraps her arms around my shoulders and gives me a squeeze. "Remember to eat a good-sized breakfast every morning. I don't care how much time you say you'll have; you need to eat to keep up your energy."

"I will."

"And you make sure Rory and Hart eat. Those boys need someone to look out for them."

"I'll remind them."

"And make sure you get enough sleep. I can already see the circles under your eyes." Ralda reaches up and pinches my cheeks. "I want to see a smile on your face before you leave."

I oblige and give her a second hug. "I'll miss you, Ralda. I hope you will have a pot of stew ready when I get back."

"You know I will," she says.

While I thought I would never feel the love of parents again, both Terrick and Ralda have proven that others can love you as if you were their own, if you let them. While they will never completely replace my parents, they have provided the care and guidance I have needed through my youth and early adult years. I owe them for their dedication to see me grow into the man I've become.

Marlow stands to the side of the crowd, leaning against a building. He gives me a nod and a wave. Despite our arguments in our childhood, we have since become good friends. Often, he joins Rory, Hart and me up by the viewpoint and we dream about a peaceful life in the village… before we throw stones at our rooftop targets. Marlow often spends his time helping at the market and works with Ralda to tend to the sick. He has said he wants to save as many lives as he can and the best place for him to do that is by helping the injured. He has done well in his role.

And then there is Corin, who pushes through the crowd and holds out a package covered in white cloth.

"To remember me by," she says as I take it from her.

The memory of the day I rescued her as a child hasn't faded in her mind. She obsessed over me and frequents construction sites to offer me water. No matter how often I protest and reject her, she doesn't give up. I have learned to live with it and act oblivious as much as possible, doing nothing to encourage her behavior. I believe it's working.

But I understand not being able to let go. The memory of the girl from my dream as a child hasn't faded either. Now and then, she returns to my dreams and we run through the fields of the upper valley. I am still no closer to figuring out who she is, or where she is. All I know is, I haven't met her yet. Her voice matches none of the girls in the village.

I have tried not to let my imaginary girl keep me from considering any of the young ladies here, but my dreams have set the bar. I have spent time with one or two girls. None are as sacrificial or brave as my mother or as I imagine the girl must be and so, I lose interest. While I don't know what the future holds, I hope I meet the girl from my dreams soon. She can't hide forever.

"Give them all one last hug!" Terrick shouts over the crowd.

Corin steps forward but Ralda intercepts her, much to my appreciation.

"Take care of yourself," Ralda says.

"I will do my best."

Ralda grabs Terrick's arm and wipes her tears on his sleeve. He looks down at her and smiles.

"Colfar will be fine," Terrick says, reassuringly. "You'd better get going if you want to get the distance in today."

I nod and grip Terrick's shoulder one last time.

This is it. We are leaving.

My legs felt weak with anxiety and my stomach flutters with excitement. I pull the strap of my pack tight over my shoulder and raise my arm in the air. My team assembles around me and we begin our march out of the village. The crowd cheers. They trust in us and believe we will be successful. I am choosing to believe they are right.

In only a few days, we will reach the Great Plateau where the Nadeens wait for us. We must keep a good pace to make it on time, but we will get there, and we will return with a signed treaty in our hands. I will finish the work my father started and will see this through.

"How are you feeling?" Rory asks. He gives my back a slap.

"I'm feeling good."

"How about you, Hart?"

Hart looks at Rory and pulls on his pack. "I'm not looking forward to the hike. It's already hot. I think there's a rock in my shoe."

His complaining has already begun. It will be a long journey, but not as long as the journey my village has been on to reach this moment.

The cheers of the crowd ring in my ears. My thoughts shift to the day my father left to meet with the Nadeens. Even then, the people were full of hope. Today, they still are as they watch us make the same trek as my father. I remember what it felt like to watch him walk away. To want to see his face one last time. Maybe there is someone in that crowd who wants to see my face again. I know I want to see their faces again.

I slow and allow my team to march on ahead. My heart races in my chest and my throat tightens. I am leaving my family behind. They aren't my family in a traditional sense, but they are the people who love me.

Slowly, I turn back to raise my hand and wave. Eagerly, people wave back. There are too many to count. I'm sure they wanted their loved ones to acknowledge them one last time, but I have… for them… and for me. We've made it through dark days together.

This is the start of a new beginning. Today, there is hope that things will be different… and they will be.

I believe it. Because we never lost hope.

ALSO BY C. A. EDWARDS

Read the continuation of the Elta Series.

A Hope of Peace

A Shot at Peace

A Bridge to Peace

A Fight for Peace - Coming Soon

Watch for new titles by C.A. Edwards by visiting www.
caedwardsbooks.com

GIVE A REVIEW

Reviews go a long way to help authors. They help other readers find books they may want to read.

Help spread the word about this series by leaving an online review where you purchased this book and by telling your friends.

Thank you for reading. I look forward to bringing you more great stories in the near future.

ABOUT THE AUTHOR

CHERYL EDWARDS has been a creative force from her youngest days. After spending her childhood creating and performing on stage, she developed a love for storytelling. She now lives on the Prairies of Canada with her husband and six sons. Cheryl writes the stories she loves while raising her family and pursuing a professional career.

www.caedwardsbooks.com

www.ingramcontent.com/pod-product-compliance
Lightning Source LLC
LaVergne TN
LVHW091133080826
845145LV00008B/2132

* 9 7 8 0 9 9 5 3 3 8 4 6 3 *